ESME KERR

KNIGHT'S HADDON

Mischief at MIDNIGHT

Chicken House

2 Palmer Street, Frome, Somerset BA11 1DS
www.doublecluck.com

Text © Esme Kerr 2015
First published in Great Britain in 2015
Chicken House
2 Palmer Street
Frome, Somerset BA11 1DS
United Kingdom
www.doublecluck.com

Cover and interior artwork and design by Helen Crawford-White
Typeset by Dorchester Typesetting Group Ltd
Printed and bound in Great Britain by CPI Group (UK) Ltd, Croydon, CR0 4YY
The paper used in this Chicken House book is made from wood grown in
sustainable forests.

1 3 5 7 9 10 8 6 4 2

British Library Cataloguing in Publication data available.

ISBN 978-1-909489-00-4
eISBN 978-1-910002-65-0

*For Tipu and Freya and
Foldy-in-the-middle*

Homesick for School

'How was your holiday?'

'Brillopad. Yours?'

'Topsical. Except we got snowed in for New Year.'

'That sounds fun.'

'Not really. We were meant to go to Paris.'

'*Tant pis* Paree! France is boring. Look at Sally's tan – she went to Jamaica.'

Sally made a face. 'It felt weird being on the beach in January. I wished we'd gone skiing.'

There was a murmur of sympathy through the dormitory. Everyone agreed that skiing beat the beach at New Year – everyone except Edie, who sat on her bed saying nothing. She hated the first afternoon of term, when the holiday conversations had to be got through.

'Where did you go, Edie?' Alice asked.

'I went to Folly Farm, to my cousins,' Edie said, hoping she wouldn't be asked to expand.

'Better than staying with Fothy, I expect?' said Sally.

Edie shrugged. Everyone knew that she sometimes spent her school holidays with Miss Fotheringay – the headmistress – and she sensed they all felt sorry for her on account of it. But they could never guess how much Edie preferred her times with the headmistress to her holidays in Devon with her relations and she would never admit it.

Anastasia was the only one she had told how much she hated going back to Folly Farm – to Aunt Sophia who never seemed to notice she was there, and her bullying cousin Lyle, who always did. Edie had spoken to Anastasia on the phone only a few days ago and told her how desperate things had been. 'I'm going to tell Papa that in future you must spend Christmas with us,' Anastasia had said firmly. Edie remembered how comforting and yet strangely out of place Anastasia's voice had sounded, speaking from far away in Moscow as Edie had stood in the cold, filthy kitchen at Folly Farm. She couldn't wait to see her. But Anastasia was always the last to arrive at the beginning of term.

'Any decent prezzies?' Sally persisted.

Edie blushed.

'At least you were in the country, instead of boring old London,' Rose said quickly. 'When I grow up I'm going to be a vet, and have—'

'Your very own farm with horses and pigs and chicken and sheep,' Sally and Alice laughed together.

~ 2 ~

'Boring snoring,' said Phoebe, who was slouched on the window seat, eating a chocolate bar. 'This must be the tenth—' She was silenced by a sudden commotion at the door.

'Hello, everybody! Are we all in this dorm together? What fun!'

It was Anastasia, trailing bags and looking like a china doll with her bright eyes and cheeks, and her dark hair tumbling over a fur tippet. There was a quick round of hugging, with Anastasia saving Edie to last, and squeezing her hand as she perched beside her on a bed strewn with unpacking.

'I see your maths hasn't improved over the holidays,' Rose said teasingly. 'How could seven of us fit into a four-bed dorm?'

'Head to toe?' Anastasia suggested.

'Belinda, Phoebe and me are across the corridor, with some mystery new girl,' said Rose. 'Come on, Bee, we'd better work out which beds we want before she shows up.'

Alice and Sally went to inspect their friends' quarters, leaving Edie and Anastasia alone.

'I picked these two for us,' said Edie, indicating her bed and the one next to it.

'And you've kept the one under the window for me,' Anastasia said, hugging her. 'Oh, thank you, Edie!'

Edie smiled. She knew how much Anastasia minded about such details.

'Are you all right, Edie? You don't look it,' Anastasia said, throwing herself voluptuously on to the narrow bed, and raising a critical eye from the pillow.

'I'm fine. It's good to be back. It's just—'

'Everyone banging on about their "brillopad" holidays?' Anastasia asked.

'I don't even mind that. I just get embarrassed when people ask me about Folly. I don't know what to say.'

'You could always try the truth.'

'I know. But then I'd have to admit that I preferred staying with Fothy and everyone would tease me about being her pet.'

Anastasia looked thoughtful. 'Maybe you shouldn't mind that so much, Edie. I mean, you are her pet—' Then: 'Hey!' she cried, as Edie leant forward as if to pummel her. 'I didn't mean it badly. I'm lots of people's pet. Being a pet is cool.'

'Which makes you freezing,' Edie replied.

'Far from being freezing, I am actually boiling hot,' Anastasia said, sitting up and tugging off her coat. 'Which reminds me,' she went on, as she removed her fur tippet and draped it round Edie's neck. 'This is for you.'

'But – but you can't give me this!'

'Why not? I bought it for you in Moscow, silly. I only wore it because it would have got crushed in my suit-case. Do you like it? It is real, you know.'

'I – yes, yes of course,' said Edie, stroking it uncertainly.

Anastasia smiled. 'Papa thought you might be anti-fur. He says lots of English people are boring about that sort of thing. But I told him you weren't like that. Oh,

Edie, look in the mirror – it really suits you!'

Edie tried to seem pleased, but she thought the sleek tippet draped over her brown school tunic had the look of something alarmingly alive. She was relieved when she heard Matron's voice at the door, giving her an excuse to snatch it off.

'Hello, let's see now, who have we here? Anastasia Stolonov, at last? Just who I'm looking for. How are you, dear? Good, good welcome back. Now, let's see, are you unpacked yet? From the looks of things I would say not. Excellent news, excellent. There's been a mix-up, dearie, you're not in this dormitory, you're in Charlbury with Rose and Belinda and Phoebe.'

Matron stood foursquare in the doorway, looking at the girls over her spectacles, then back to the sheet of instructions in her hand. Her expression was warm, but changed when both girls raged at her at once.

'What do you mean, a mix-up? We've always shared a dorm!'

'We can't be separated!'

'It's not fair! It must be a mistake! You can't force us!'

'Quiet! That's quite enough cheek from you,' Matron retorted. 'If you wish to make a complaint, make it to Miss Fotheringay, not to me. But I can assure you her instructions were quite specific. You know how much trouble she takes over her dormitory cast lists.'

Anastasia's brow darkened. 'But why would she do that to us? She's just being mean on purpose.'

'She's the boss,' said Matron. 'Ask her. Now, hurry up, please. I have better things to do on the first day of term than argue with obstreperous second years.'

'I'm not going anywhere,' said Anastasia, sitting firmly on her bed. 'We're on strike, aren't we, Edie?'

'Strike about what?' asked Alice, reappearing with Sally.

'They're trying to move me into Charlbury!' said Anastasia.

'Charlbury?' Sally frowned. 'Then who's coming in here?'

'A new girl,' Matron replied briskly. 'Janet Stone.'

'That can't be right,' said Sally, joining in. 'Her name's on the door of Charlbury. Rose and Belinda were wondering who she was. Do you know anything about her, Matron?'

'Nothing at all,' Matron said firmly. 'Now get moving, Anastasia, or you'll find yourself spending the first night of term in the sick room.'

'I don't care if I do,' said Anastasia mulishly, but Edie could hear the choke in her voice.

When Matron had gone she tried to reassure her. 'Charlbury's only across the corridor, Ansti, and I'll sneak into your dorm every night. And at least this way we'll definitely get to be together in the summer – Fothy wouldn't dare separate us two terms running.'

'Fothy would dare do anything,' Anastasia said, letting out a sob.

Edie felt guilty. Anastasia clearly cared much more about the sleeping arrangements than she did. Her days as Anastasia's secret protector were long gone, but sometimes Edie was struck to see how much her friend still relied on her.

'Shall we go and see Fothy?' Edie said quietly. 'We can now, before Matron comes back.'

'You go,' Anastasia said, pulling a photograph from her case and placing it firmly on the bedside table. 'You can always get your way with her.'

'Well, my dear, I wondered when I was going to be honoured with a visit,' Miss Fotheringay said, rising from her desk and gesturing Edie to come and stand beside her.

'I'm sorry,' Edie faltered. 'I was going to come, only—'

'You had your friends to say hello to first,' said Miss Fotheringay, taking Edie's hands in hers and looking at her full in the face. 'I understand.'

No, you don't, thought Edie, who had secretly been longing to see the headmistress. When the others were at tea she had prowled about the corridors, hoping Miss Fotheringay might appear. But despite all the time they had spent alone together in the holidays, in term time Edie didn't dare knock on the headmistress's door without a reason.

Miss Fotheringay let go of Edie's hands. 'You haven't just come to say hello,' she said.

Edie immediately felt wrong-footed.

'Something is bothering you, Edith. Tell me what it is.'

'It's about your dormitory cast list,' Edie said, blushing.

Miss Fotheringay inclined her head.

'Matron came and said there'd been a mistake and that

Anastasia had to go in with Rose and Belinda, and—' Edie gave up, squirming at how babyish it sounded.

Miss Fotheringay frowned. 'That's right, I think. Yes, that's what I arranged.' She looked at Edie expectantly, as if challenging her to say more.

'Anastasia's not at all happy,' Edie said, blaming her friend.

Miss Fotheringay's mouth set in a firm line. 'Then Anastasia should come and talk to me.'

'That's what I thought, but she said it would be better—' Edie stopped, sensing she was making things worse. 'What I meant was—'

'Yes, Edith?'

Edie felt the familiar crumpling of her stomach at the cool, clear tone in which Miss Fotheringay spoke her name. All the other teachers had started calling her Edie, even the Man, but with Miss Fotheringay she was still Edith. 'That was the name your mother chose for you, Edith,' Miss Fotheringay had said once. 'I see no reason to give you another one.' And Edie was glad.

'You are not Anastasia's minder, Edith,' Miss Fotheringay said now. 'You can let her stand up for herself sometimes.'

'Yes, but—'

'You are not joined at the hip, Edith. Or are you?'

'No, it's just – just that we'd both prefer to sleep in the same dormitory, that's all,' Edie said feebly.

Miss Fotheringay smiled. 'And there's nothing wrong with that. But I am afraid, Edith, I am not going to let you pit your childish preference against a greater good.'

'What greater good?' Edie asked, baffled.

'At last!' Miss Fotheringay said, clapping her hands. 'I was afraid you would never ask!' She poured herself a drink, and sank on to the sofa. 'Sit!' she commanded, patting the seat beside her. 'A new girl is joining the school,' she went on, looking at Edie squarely. 'I have agreed to take her at short notice, and I felt I could depend on you to look after her.'

'Me and Anastasia could look after her together,' Edie said earnestly.

'Anastasia and I,' Miss Fotheringay corrected her. 'And you must let me be the judge of how helpful Anastasia would be in this instance. She is not used to looking after people.'

'She looks after me!'

Miss Fotheringay arched an eyebrow. 'The new girl, Janet, is going to find it difficult arriving in the middle of the school year,' she continued. 'And her home circumstances are not easy. I wasn't at all sure whether I should take her. Then I thought about you, Edith, and I did not think I could, in all conscience, refuse haven to a child who might be in as great a need as you were, when you first came to me.'

Edie remembered her first visit to Miss Fotheringay's office more than a year ago, when she had sat frozen on the sofa, hypnotised by Miss Fotheringay's searchlight gaze. Edie shook herself. That girl no longer existed. She was stronger now.

'Now tell me, Edith, how was Folly?'

Edie shrugged, but she could feel her throat tightening.

'My poor child.'

'It wasn't that bad,' Edie said quickly. 'I just felt – homesick . . . for school.'

She hadn't meant to say it. She had thought during the holidays how strange it would sound to say it out loud – 'homesick for school' – and had imagined discussing it with Anastasia, no one else. But Miss Fotheringay always had a way of making Edie say more than she intended.

'I'm sorry I couldn't take you with me to my parents,' Miss Fotheringay said. 'They both missed you.' As she spoke she got up and walked to the window, then pulled back the curtain and stood staring pensively into the night.

'How – how is your father?' Edie asked cautiously. She knew Mr Fotheringay had not been well.

The headmistress did not look round. 'You have heard about the Prefects' Tower?' she said, changing the subject.

'No,' Edie replied.

The Prefects' Tower stood in the woods just outside the boundary of the park. It was a proper hideaway, with bunk beds and a kitchen, and a turret window from which you could spy out over the treetops – but as its name suggested, only prefects were allowed to use it.

The tower was where Edie and Anastasia had taken refuge when they were trying to escape Anastasia's kidnappers. But no one referred to that now.

'It won't be the Prefects' Tower much longer,' Miss Fotheringay said, gazing out in its direction. 'It's been sold, and is to be converted into a house. There's been quite a fuss about it in the village – they're going to cut down nearly an acre of trees to build a proper road up to it and make a garden and they'll have to build a new bridge over the river too.'

Edie looked at her in astonishment. She knew the tower did not belong to the school. It belonged to the Greyling family, whose daughter had been head girl at Knight's Haddon last year. The Greylings owned most of the neighbouring land, but they had always let the school have use of the tower, even before their daughter arrived there. All the Knight's Haddon girls looked on it as their own. 'But – but it can't be sold,' she said, shocked.

'Don't be so silly, Edith. The tower is private property. Helen's family had a right to sell it, and now they have done so. We should just consider ourselves lucky to have had the use of it for so long.'

'But – but they can't just cut down the trees!' Edie said.

'On the contrary, the council has given permission for it,' Miss Fotheringay said. 'Some people aren't happy – there's been some petition going around, I gather, but at this stage any protest will be an exercise in futility.'

'Who's bought it?' Edie asked, curious.

Miss Fotheringay closed the curtains with an air of impatience. 'That will emerge.' She turned, and looked at Edie searchingly. 'I sometimes wondered how you would have felt about using the tower when – if – you become a prefect. It might have felt strange for you after what you went through there.'

Edie blushed. The kidnap was so seldom talked about, that even with Miss Fotheringay she felt awkward when it was.'Your father?' she said again, to change the subject. 'Is he very ill?'

'He was, then he rallied enough to ask after you, and to request that I make you a present of this,' the headmistress replied, handing Edie a brown paper package that had been lying on the desk.

Edie unwrapped it to find a copy of *Macbeth, a Play by William Shakespeare*. It looked very old, with gold lettering, and a leather cover crumbling at the seams. When Edie opened it she found a bookplate with a school crest, and an inscription to Michael Fotheringay, 'For First Prize in History, 1945'. Edie gave a smile of surprised pleasure.

'He knew you would be reading it later this term, and wanted you to have his copy,' Miss Fotheringay said brusquely. 'Now run along, and see if they've left any supper for you.'

Mystery Newgirl

Edie was glad that Anastasia had not seen how easily defeated she had been in the headmistress's study. Edie avoided her at supper, and when the others went off to swap tuck in the common room, she stole back to the dormitory on her own. It was gloomy, with only a dim bedside lamp left on, but the lighting suited Edie's mood. She sat down on her bed and stared at the floor, deep in thought.

'Er . . . do people, like, not even say hello to each other at this school? Or have I done something wrong already?'

Edie jumped, and turning round she saw a figure hunched in the next bed.

'Oh, I didn't see you. Are you – the new girl?'

'Yeah. I do actually have a name as well.'

'I'm sorry, I wasn't thinking, it's only because you gave

me such a fright,' Edie said, realizing how clumsy she must have sounded. 'You're Janet, aren't you?'

'Mmm,' the girl replied. 'Famous already, am I?'

'N-no,' Edie said. 'Matron mentioned it. And it's written on the door.'

'Not this door,' Janet observed. 'Which is a bit weird. But I was told there'd been a mix-up which didn't completely surprise me as the school only agreed to take me the day before yesterday – worse luck.'

'You – didn't want to come here then?' Edie asked stupidly, peering at the new arrival through the half-light. Edie's main impression was of size – of arms and legs going in every direction, like a giant doll that had been tossed from a pram, and landed spread-eagled on the bed. Eventually a face appeared, wide and white, with eyes peering from behind a pair of thick-rimmed spectacles and a tangle of black hair. Even her voice was heavy, the words dropping from her mouth, weary, weighted with indignation.

'You bet I didn't. Does anyone? No mobiles, no internet, no nothing. What's it all about? Even people who live in tree-houses have mobiles. As for a school without computers, I've never heard of anything so stupid.'

Edie smiled. Miss Fotheringay's views on the modern world were always a keen talking point among new girls. Virtually all electrical gadgets were banned at Knight's Haddon. Only the sixth-formers had access to the coveted computer room, and woe betide any girl who tried squirrelling a mobile on to the premises – Miss Mannering always managed to unearth them during her dreaded dormitory inspections.

'You soon get used to it,' she said in a friendly voice, remembering her own bewilderment at the rules in her first term.

'I won't,' murmured the girl. 'One term max, then I'm out of here.'

'That's exactly what I thought, but then—'

'Then here you are, stuck in and making the most of it,' said Janet. 'Well, I'll do better. I'm going to get myself chucked out. Shouldn't be difficult if it's as strict as all that.'

Edie looked at her quizzically. 'Why did you come here if you feel like that?'

Janet glared. 'Do you think I had a choice? My mother got a job in New York, editing some stupid magazine, so I got packed off to prison. I would have stayed with my dad if he wasn't so—'

'What?' Edie asked.

'Pathetic,' Janet said bitterly. 'But I suppose boarding schools depend on useless parents. What are yours like?'

'My mother's dead,' Edie said simply.

Janet let out a long whistle. 'And your dad?'

'Also dead.'

Janet let out a long whistle. 'An orphan – cool!'

Edie was taken aback. Most people were so embarrassed when they discovered she was an orphan they didn't know where to look.

'Lucky you,' Janet went on, unabashed. 'I'd love to be free of my parents!'

'But you *are* free of them – you're at boarding school,'

Edie pointed out. Then: 'Hey – what's that?' she whispered, as Janet produced a can of drink.

Janet laughed. 'You needn't sound so worried – it's only lemonade. D'you want a swig?'

But as the can passed between them it slipped and spilled on to the bed, which was still strewn with Anastasia's clothes.

'Ah – I'm sorry. Is this your coat?' Janet asked casually, holding up a splattered garment for Edie to inspect.

'No,' said Edie querulously. 'It's Anastasia's. And that's her bed. Or at least it was. Maybe you should wait until she's collected her things until you take it over.'

'Who's Anastasia?' Janet yawned.

'I am. Who are *you*, more to the point, and why are you both sitting here in the dark?' came an indignant voice. Next moment the room burst into light, and Edie turned to see Anastasia glowering at Janet from the doorway.

Edie's eyes moved uneasily between them, glad at least that Anastasia's anger wasn't turned on her. Now that she could see her clearly, Edie was struck by how much older Janet looked, more like a fifth than a second year, and despite her spectacles there was something wild in her appearance, with her pale skin and matted hair. She lolled nonchalantly on her pillow, seeming quite undeterred by Anastasia's presence, but then she suddenly leapt from the bed and hurled the tippet from her with a shriek: 'Aagh! What is it? It's a rat!'

'How dare you!' shouted Anastasia, snatching the fur from the floor. 'Hey? It's wet! What have you done?

Who are you? Get off my bed!'

'Anastasia!' Edie hissed, her eyes gesturing desperately at the door – but Anastasia was facing the other way, and had not seen the headmistress appear.

'Anastasia, come with me please,' Miss Fotheringay said, in a voice which not even Anastasia dared to disobey.

'I tried,' Edie mouthed, as Anastasia looked back in fury from the doorway.

'So what happens now?' asked Janet, after lights out.

'We go to sleep,' said Sally.

'Boring,' said Janet.

'Only the boring get bored,' said Alice.

'Boring,' repeated Janet. 'Edie?'

No answer. Janet sat up and threw a pillow at the bed beside her. 'Edie's done a runner!' she called out, excitedly.

'She's probably snuck out to say goodnight to Anastasia,' giggled Sally.

'They're sort-of married,' explained Alice.

'Interesting,' said Janet, who very soon began to snore.

Edie's dressing-gown was a cast off from Aunt Sophia, and was so long it trailed about her feet like a wedding train. She had to hoist it off the floor as she crept across the corridor, and slipped into Anastasia's dormitory. There was not a sound, but she knew at once that the members of Charlbury were wide awake. The curtain had been pushed back, and the moonlight lay in a puddle on the floor. Edie stood still for a moment, adjusting her eyes, and saw that two of the other three beds were empty. The third looked as though it had the Loch Ness monster under its blankets. The monster, sensing a new presence in the room, was holding its breath.

'It's only me,' Edie whispered. 'Coast is clear.'

'Can we trust her?' came a muffled voice.

'It might be an impostor,' said another, as Anastasia broke ranks and peeked out from under the blanket.

'Oh, Edie,' she sighed. 'I missed you so much that Belinda and Rose had to come and cheer me up.'

'And did we succeed?' asked Rose, emerging from the tangle of blankets to sit on one side of Anastasia, while Belinda took the other.

'Total failure,' said Anastasia in a voice of mock mournfulness. 'But thank you for trying.'

Edie heard the unspoken accusation. 'I'm sorry, Anastasia,' she said. 'But Fothy just went on about the new girl needing to be looked after.'

'She didn't look as if she needed much looking after to me!' Anastasia said indignantly. 'But if Fothy thinks she needs someone to hold her hand, then why couldn't we have done it together?'

'That's what I said, but—'

'But?'

'Oh, I don't know,' Edie said, defeated. 'You know what Fothy's like, Ansti. She probably just wants to see if we can survive in separate rooms for a term.'

'She better not try that on us,' said Belinda, looking

solemnly at Rose.

'What would you do if she did?' asked Anastasia.

There was a pause, while Rose and Belinda considered the question.

'I don't know,' said Rose, curling into a tiny ball on the edge of the bed, her knees hugged under her chin. 'But something pretty big!'

'No, you wouldn't. You're terrified of her. Everyone is, admit it,' said Phoebe.

'Maybe, but I'd still stand up to her all right if she tried to separate me from Belinda,' Rose replied.

Anastasia said nothing, but looked at Edie pointedly as the other girls returned to their beds.

Edie felt a secret flash of defiance. Anastasia had been unpopular when she had first arrived at Knight's Haddon, but after the kidnap attempt in her first term she had become the school's pet princess, and everyone wanted to be her friend. *Fothy's right*, Edie thought. *Anastasia can look after herself.* Then – 'Here, I brought you this,' she said, dropping a small, heavy object into Anastasia's lap.

'But, Edie, it's Birdy! He belongs to you!' Anastasia protested.

'I thought we could share him,' Edie replied. 'He can fly between our dorms at night without a sound – and if the Man tries to catch him, he'll peck her in the eye!'

Anastasia giggled. Edie knew her love of fairy tales and superstition, and she was clearly delighted with the idea of Birdy acting as a secret midnight messenger between the dormitories.

'I'm sorry to be grumpy, Edie. It's just that the whole term's got off to a wrong start,' Anastasia said, wriggling under her covers. 'What's with the dressing gown, by the way?' she asked, casting a disapproving eye over Edie's voluminous scarlet fleece. 'Pretty hideoso.'

'I know,' said Edie, laughing. 'I said I needed one and Aunt Sophia just produced it from her cupboard. She said it was too ugly for her, but that it would "do for school". But it won't do at all, I realize now. It's impossibly long on me.'

'Hideoso *and* impracticale,' said Anastasia. 'I'll tell Papa to get you something proper in Paris. He's there now and— Hey, does everyone know it's my birthday on Saturday?'

'This Saturday?' Belinda piped excitedly from the next bed. Last year Anastasia's father had sent an enormous pink cake, and enough sweets and chocolates for Anastasia to host a midnight feast every weekend for the rest of term. The bounty meant that Anastasia's birthday this year was an eagerly anticipated event.

Edie nodded. 'What's happening?' she asked.

'He was going to take me out to lunch,' Anastasia explained. 'It was all fixed up, and he'd got Fothy to agree that I could bring three friends, but then just as he was dropping me back this evening Papa took a call, and I don't know what it was about because he was talking in German – but whatever it was it was something important, and now he can't come! Oh, it's so annoying! I could have chosen anyone I liked and we could've all gone to the Old Stoke and made complete pigs of ourselves.'

'Who would you have asked?' Belinda wondered, as if wanting to act out the delicious scene in her mind.

'Well, Edie, of course,' Anastasia said, planning her pretend guest list. 'And then, seeing as we're all in the dorm together, I suppose I'd have asked you, and—'

Edie gave her a nudge, gesturing towards the silent figure in the corner bed. Edie was sure Anastasia wouldn't have wanted Phoebe to be included in the party, but it seemed hurtful to exclude her from the feast, even if it was only an imaginary one.

'I couldn't have come, anyway,' Phoebe yawned. 'My cousin's getting married, and I'm being allowed out for the day.'

'Oh well, that's a pity – then I suppose I would have chosen Belinda and Rose,' Anastasia said, letting her fancy fly away again. 'And Papa said we could have eaten anything we wanted, and then he'd have taken us to the cinema – he'd got Fothy to agree we didn't have to be back at school until supper time. But now I have to cancel the whole thing!'

'What do you mean, you have to cancel it?' asked Rose. She was hunched in bed with her diary propped on her knees, her face peering ghost-like through her torchlight. 'Has your father told Fothy it's off?'

Anastasia shrugged. 'He told me to tell her.'

'Ansti, don't say anything!' Rose hissed. 'If she's already agreed to it, then why tell her it's off? Was your father going to come to the school himself?'

'No,' Anastasia said hesitantly. 'He was going to send a car to pick everyone up and take us the ten miles to the restaurant. His plan was to fly in from Paris that morning and meet us there.'

'Then we can still go!' Rose said in a thrilled voice. 'He'll have cancelled the car but we can just order another one – Fothy will never know.'

'But how would we pay?' Edie said practically. 'And besides, the Old Stoke probably wouldn't let us eat in the dining room without a grown-up.'

'We won't go to the Old Stoke. Restaurants are boring anyway,' said Rose.

'Speak for yourself,' said Belinda. 'Anyway, where shall we go instead?'

'To the gypsy horse fair,' Rose said firmly.

'What's that?' asked Edie.

'What do you think it is?' Rose sighed. 'It's a horse fair run by travellers. It happens every year at Parley's Head, only about ten miles from here. I've been before with my godmother and it was such fun!'

'Yes!' shouted Anastasia, clapping her hands.

'But Anastasia, you must be mad!' Edie looked at her aghast. 'You know what your father's like about security. If he hears about us going there without telling anyone he'll have the school closed down!'

'No he won't, because he won't find out. And nor will Fothy,' Anastasia added, in a determined voice. 'Now, are you in or are you out?'

Edie felt three pairs of eyes fix on her in the moon-light.

'In, of course,' she said, sounding stouter than she felt.

Anastasia's Rules

Edie was secretly pleased that Miss Fotheringay had trusted her to look after Janet, and she had no intention of letting the headmistress down. But Janet made it clear she wanted no looking after at all. She didn't seem to feel any of the usual new girl's anxieties about meal times, or about which bells signified which lessons, or remembering which parts of the school were out of bounds – and all attempts by Edie to explain the rules were met with a roll of the eyes.

Edie had never known anyone collect so many order marks for lateness or untidiness, or for being in the wrong part of the school at the wrong time. 'Now you'll be gated on Saturday,' she said ruefully, as Janet slunk in late for lunch.

'Let them try,' Janet said, flicking a pea across the table.

On Wednesday Edie ambushed Janet after breakfast so that she could show her the way to the Man's classroom, where they were due for their first history lesson of the term. 'You *can't* be late for the Man,' Edie warned, steering her down the corridor. 'And you mustn't speak until you're invited into the conversation, but after that you're allowed to call out,' she went on, explaining the Man's peculiar methods. 'She's not nearly such a dragon when she's teaching. In fact, I'd say she was—'

Janet stopped walking, and looked at her with an expression of derision.

'What?' said Edie, looking at her watch.

'It's just . . . the way you all talk about the teachers and the rules. Anyone would think that you were glad to be here.'

Edie blushed. She *was* glad to be there. But there were reasons for that – reasons which didn't bear going into as they stood in the narrow corridor, with girls rushing past them on either side.

'Please, Janet,' she said. 'We'll be late.'

'Hey, sister,' said Janet, leaning into Edie's face. 'Far be it from me to drag you down. I've left something in the dormitory. I'll catch you up.'

'No you won't,' wailed Edie. 'You won't know where to go!'

'I'll ask,' said Janet, and then she was gone.

Edie wondered whether to follow. Her instructions were to help Newgirl learn the ropes. But what if Newgirl refused to learn?

'You're with me, I think,' said Miss Mannering, sweeping up behind her. 'Chop chop, you should be at your desk by now.'

'Sorry,' Edie murmured. 'I was waiting—'

'Humph,' said Miss Mannering crisply. 'Waiting's for wastrels. Lateness is a vice—'

'Which loses wars,' Edie finished the sentence, trotting to keep up.

The rest of the class were sitting at their desks when Edie and Miss Mannering arrived and the lesson began at once, with the teacher picking up where she had left off the previous term, as though the holidays had never taken place.

'Let's begin with a definition of democracy,' said the Man, quietly ticking off names on a list. 'Phoebe?'

'Rule by the people?' Phoebe ventured.

'Correct,' said the Man. 'Rule by the people by means of the vote. Meanwhile,' she continued with a playful wave of the register, 'my own personal register of electors shows we are one short.'

Janet arrived as though on cue, with her shirt untucked and her tie slung back over her shoulder.

'Janet Stone, welcome to my class,' Miss Mannering said, and motioned to an empty desk in the front row.

'Hi,' Janet replied, slumping into her chair.

Everyone looked at the Man in suspense, but for once even the formidable deputy seemed lost for words – or was saving them for later.

Maths followed a similar pattern. While the others struggled over algebra, Janet spent the first half of the lesson hidden behind her ponytail of tangled hair – 'looking for split ends,' she explained to Edie afterwards – until Mr Robinson, a nervous young teacher who had joined the school the previous term, invited her to come to the front of the class and write an answer to the question he had just chalked up on the board.

'Why are you picking on me?' Janet asked sulkily.

'Because I don't think you've been paying attention,' Mr Robinson replied.

Janet scraped back her chair, and walked to the front of the class with her shoulders swaying. 'What's the point trying to work out the answer when the question doesn't make sense?' she said, and proceeded to insert a missing bracket into Mr Robinson's equation.

'That was awesome,' said Belinda later, over tea. 'He looked so embarrassed! Oh, Janet, you should have seen him when you were walking back to your desk – his face was like strawberry jam!'

'I felt sorry for him,' said Anastasia. 'He's so shy, and sometimes I think he's frightened of us. Do you remember that time he was on supper duty last term and no one would stop talking during Grace – he looked as though he was going to cry.'

There was a murmur of agreement, but Janet scoffed: 'Mr Robinson doesn't have feelings. He's more sheep than man. Baa! Baa! Baa!' she bleated, mimicking the maths teacher's ponderous expression as he peered round the class, rubbing his forehead. 'Baa! Baa! Baa!'

There was a burst of laughter as everyone recognized Mr Robinson's peculiar gestures – but Anastasia remained stony-faced. Edie wondered if she really felt sorry for the maths teacher – or whether it was simply Janet's skill at mimicry that had upset her. Acting was Anastasia's passion, and she was used to getting the lead parts in school plays. 'You're one of the best actors the school's ever seen,' the head girl had said to her in their first term, and no one in the second year would dispute it. They were all proud to have Anastasia representing the lower school on stage. But did Anastasia now feel she might have met her match?

'I don't see the point of being here if you're so determined to hate it,' Anastasia said coolly.

Edie felt the same, and she suspected the other girls did too, but nonetheless there was something in Anastasia's tone which made everyone uneasy.

'You're quite right,' Janet replied, fixing Anastasia with a level gaze. 'There isn't any point at all to my being here, which is why I'm determined to hate it.'

'But you could decide to give it a go, couldn't you?' asked Sally in a puzzled voice. 'Lots of people would give their eye teeth for a Knight's Haddon education.'

'It's true,' said Alice. 'And you've got to go to school somewhere. It's the law.'

'It's the law—' Janet parroted the words in a mocking voice. 'You sound like my mother. Anyway, it isn't true.'

'What isn't true?'

'The law doesn't say that children have to be in school. As long as parents can prove that their children are being educated the government can't insist that it happens in a classroom. Most children go to school because their parents don't want them around. And at boarding school that's triply true.'

'My parents would love to have me at home, but the local school didn't do Latin,' said Alice primly.

'Latin, eh?' said Janet sarcastically. 'You won't get far in the world without that.'

'What's wrong with learning other languages?'

'Nothing. But why not learn a language that people actually speak? At Knight's Haddon there's this weird obsession with what people don't think any more, or do or say. Computers are out, dead languages are in. I just don't get it.'

'You will,' said Alice.

'No, I won't. And you don't get it either. You've been brainwashed into thinking you're getting a privileged education when in fact boarding school is just a place where selfish parents dump their unwanted children.'

'Rubbish. Speak for yourself, Newgirl.'

'Perhaps that's all I am doing,' said Janet in a quiet voice. Then she got up and walked away.

'Oh dear,' said Alice. 'I hope I didn't—'

'You didn't anything,' Sally said firmly. 'She's just weird.'

There was an awkwardness round the table, and Edie was relieved when the conversation moved on to the tower. Everyone had been outraged when Miss Fotheringay had announced at the first assembly of term that it had been sold for development, and that both the tower and the surrounding woodland were now out of bounds.

'Isn't it hideous of Helen's father, selling it off like that, without even thinking how we'd feel!'

A murmur of assent went round the group.

'I think it's outrageous,' said Belinda. 'I can't believe Helen agreed to it!'

During Helen Greyling's headship the previous year she and the other prefects had held parties at the tower, and camped there on summer weekends.

'I suppose Helen doesn't care any more, now that she's left the school,' someone said bitterly.

'But what about us?'

Everyone agreed that it was unsporting of the Greyling family to let the tower go, just because Helen had left the school.

'It's just greedy to sell,' said Rose. 'If Mr Greyling's short of money, why doesn't he sell a barn?'

'Maybe the house won't be built anyway,' said Rose. 'Matron said that her friends in the village have objected to it because of all the trees that are going to be cut down.'

'But how can they stop it? Fothy said in assembly that the building work was starting this term!'

Then, 'Oh, come on,' someone said, as the bell summoned them to prep.

Anastasia had gone noticeably silent after her confrontation with Janet at tea, and Edie noticed that she went on looking unhappy all evening.

'Are you OK?' she asked her after supper, when they found themselves alone in Anastasia's dormitory.

'Not really,' said Anastasia. 'I mean, that Janet girl—'

'Oh, please don't mind about her,' Edie said. 'I'm only trying to help her settle in.'

'Why bother? She's going to leave anyway.'

'She probably isn't going to leave.'

'Great,' Anastasia said glumly.

'Listen, you're my best friend,' Edie said earnestly. 'Nothing's going to change that.'

'Famous last words,' Anastasia replied. She picked up the glass bird from her bedside table, and sat silently a while, stroking it in her hand.

'Oh, Edie, it's not just that,' she said. 'It's the tower.'

'I know,' Edie began.

'No, you don't!' Anastasia said passionately. 'You don't know half of it! And I can't tell you! Not even you – because you'll . . . you'll tell everyone else, and they'll all hate me!'

'Hate you for what?' Edie asked, mystified.

'For everything! Oh, Edie, can't you see – it's all my fault! It's all because of me! You know how pleased I was when Papa agreed I didn't have to have a bodyguard – that I could have as normal a time at school as possible. Well, it was all a trick. He's been in conversation with Helen's father about that piece of land ever since I came here, and now he's *bought* it, and he says I can't object because he's going to build a house there, not for a body-guard but for . . . guess who for?'

'Himself?'

'No. Though that might be better. At least he's not . . . Oh, Edie, so much happened in the holidays that I haven't told you. My mother's left her horrible husband at last and wants to come and live near the school, so Papa's idea is to convert the Prefects' Tower into a house for her!'

Edie looked stunned. She thought of the conversation they'd had on the phone during the Christmas holidays, when she had been complaining about her miserable time at Folly Farm – while little guessing what was going on in Anastasia's life.

'But – but, Anastasia, I can't believe you've been keeping all this to yourself!'

'I know,' said Anastasia. 'I can't bear thinking about it. And the worst of it is I'm supposed to be pleased about Mama, and of course I am, in a way, except she's so . . . well, she gets so worried about everything and she won't stick to the rules. She never has.'

'What rules?'

'*My* rules,' said Anastasia fiercely. 'About letting me be!'

Edie and Anastasia's conversation was cut short when Belinda and Rose appeared.

'Hey, Edie!' Anastasia said, suddenly summoning a smile. 'Have you heard about Saturday? Rose has been brilliant – she's booked us a taxi to come and pick us up from the main entrance at twelve o'clock, which is the time Papa's car was going to come, so now we're all going to the fair!'

'In time for lunch!' Belinda joined in eagerly.

'But what if Fothy talks to the driver?' Edie asked. 'She'll know your father wouldn't have sent a taxi –

when he's got his own driver.'

'But that's the best part of it – Fothy won't be here!' Rose said in a thrilled voice. 'I had to go and hand in some late prep at the staff common room this afternoon, and when I was waiting Fothy and the Man came down the corridor and I heard them talking – and the gist of it was that Fothy said she was going to see her parents and could the Man be on duty.'

'The Man?' Edie groaned.

'Ha! She'll want to check every detail – and I wouldn't like to be in your shoes when she catches you out,' Phoebe yawned.

'Oh no, but it gets better!' Rose said gleefully. 'The Man said she couldn't – but that she'd ask Mr Robinson!'

Anastasia giggled. The thought of the trip seemed to have restored her. 'We could probably all go out dressed in bikinis and he wouldn't think to stop us!'

Everyone seemed delighted with the developments, but Edie still had a sense of deep unease. How could Anastasia possibly think they would get away with such a stunt? Surely she knew that all the staff had been instructed to keep an extra close watch on her following the kidnap attempt last year.

'How will we get back from the fair?' she asked practically.

Anastasia shrugged. 'Get another taxi, I guess. Oh, Edie do stop thinking of problems,' she said, her voice suddenly irritable. 'Sometimes I think you want to spoil the whole thing before it happens.'

*

Edie was in the common room, playing cards with Janet, when she was summoned to the headmistress's study.

'Well, Edith, what sort of term are you having so far?' asked Miss Fotheringay, motioning her to the sofa.

'It's fine,' Edie said, wondering if she was going to be given a dressing-down for Janet's order marks – or for her own. 'Except – except there hasn't been very much of it yet,' she added hesitantly.

'Ah, so the time is passing quickly. Then you must be having fun.'

This was not what Edie had meant, but she knew better than to make a point of it. Miss Fotheringay was happy to roll up her sleeves for a real argument, but she hated to be contradicted on small matters.

'You are not missing Anastasia too much?'

Edie looked at her warily – but there was nothing in the headmistress's expression to suggest that Edie's dormitory-hopping had been brought to her attention.

'It's a bit – a bit weird being in different dormitories,' she said.

Miss Fotheringay winced. 'If only, Edith, you could learn not to use that word—'

Edie bit her lip. Fothy had a hit list of hated words, which she claimed had been over-used into meaninglessness. 'Weird' was one of them. 'Nice' was another.

Then, changing the subject – 'How's Janet settling in?' the headmistress asked.

'I – I wouldn't call her settled exactly,' Edie answered carefully.

'No,' Miss Fotheringay agreed, with a hint of

impatience. 'The general impression seems to be that she has no interest in being here at all. Is that right?'

'I – I don't know,' said Edie slowly.

'I trust that you would tell me if you had any real cause for concern in her behaviour?' Miss Fotheringay persisted.

Edie felt on guard. Was she being asked to spy again?

'I've taken a risk with Janet. It may be that Knight's Haddon isn't the right school for her. She's an able girl who is, I fear, capable of extreme silliness. It's so important, Edith, to harness the clever ones.' Miss Fotheringay paused, as though deep in thought. Edie coughed nervously, and the headmistress shook her head and turned to her with a quick, apologetic smile. 'I didn't mean to talk about Janet when I asked you to come and see me,' she said. 'Really, I wanted to find out whether you'd like to come and see my father this Saturday. If he's well enough. Which he does seem to be at the moment.'

'Oh, yes!' Edie said eagerly – then her face fell. 'I'd have loved to, only . . . I – I can't.'

'Why not?' Miss Fotheringay asked, looking puzzled. Edie felt a flush of panic as she struggled to remember the agreed version of events. 'It's – it's Anastasia's birthday,' she said finally, her voice sounding high and forced, while her eyes sank to the floor.

'Ah, of course it is,' Miss Fotheringay said, nodding.

'I think – she said that she had permission to take four of us out to lunch at the Old Stoke,' Edie went on, picking through the facts in a faltering attempt to avoid telling any outright lies.

'Yes,' Miss Fotheringay said, throwing Edie a look which might have stopped her in her tracks had she caught it. 'I believe that was the arrangement.'

'I . . . I can't let Anastasia down on her birthday,' Edie said, her eyes fixed on the carpet. 'I'm sorry. I was going to write to your father . . . to thank him for the copy of *Macbeth*. I was waiting until I'd read it through, but perhaps I shouldn't wait – I should just write and you could take him the letter.'

'Fine,' Miss Fotheringay said abruptly, in her most headmistressy tone. 'Leave it in my pigeon-hole. Now, run along, child, it's nearly bedtime. And you must be tired,' she added pointedly, 'with all your late-night gallivanting.'

Miss Fotheringay sat silently a while after Edie had gone, listening to the footsteps retreating down the corridor. Then she rose, and picked up the telephone from her desk.

'Mummy? . . . Yes, yes, all well. But it's about Saturday . . . something's cropped up. I'm afraid I might be a bit late.'

The Man Called Stonor

Edie lay awake late on Friday night. She wished, guiltily, that she could wriggle out of the trip to the fair and go to lunch with Miss Fotheringay tomorrow instead, but Anastasia would never forgive her.

The others had been talking about the trip in fevered whispers all day, but Edie was dreading it. She knew Rose had been careful to book the taxi in her own name, making no mention of Anastasia Stolonov – but what if the driver recognized her? Anastasia's kidnap attempt had been the subject of lurid articles in all the national newspapers – and it had held the front page of the local papers for days on end. Much of the coverage had been wildly inaccurate too. Edie still felt indignant about the headline in the *Cotswold Courier* – DRUGGED RUSSIAN PRINCESS RESCUED BY POLICE IN MIDNIGHT RAID ON RUINED

TOWER – in which every single fact had been wrong.

It was Edie who had been found in the tower, undrugged, at dawn – and by Miss Fotheringay.

Anastasia was the one who had been drugged into sleep, then spirited away in a car, which was stopped by the police as her kidnappers were attempting to smuggle her on to a ferry.

But however inaccurate, the coverage had at least ensured that everyone in the village knew about Anastasia's presence in the school. And even though the papers had been prohibited from carrying her photograph, Edie sensed that the locals had all worked out which one she was. Anastasia's face was certainly well known in the village tearoom – the Blue Kettle – where the staff always greeted her by name, and she was also known in the post office.

What they were plotting for tomorrow was far more daring than the pranks any of the second years had got up to before, but Edie felt none of the others' bravado. Instead she felt an impostor, unqualified for a delinquent's role.

It was nearly midnight when Edie finally fell asleep, and on Saturday morning she had to be shaken awake by Sally. She dressed just in time for the breakfast bell, but when she went over to Charlbury she found Anastasia still in her dressing gown, languidly brushing her hair.

'Are you excited?' Anastasia asked, glancing mischievously at Edie in the mirror.

'I think we should call it off,' Edie said.

'Call it off?' Anastasia turned to her with a baffled expression. 'Edie, what do you mean?'

'We're going to get caught, Anastasia. There are so many things wrong with it as a plan. I lay awake half the night thinking about it.'

'Rubbish,' Anastasia said firmly. 'Rose is a genius strategist. It's all the dressage she does at pony camp.'

'What's dressage?'

'I'm not sure,' said Anastasia, 'but I'm pretty sure it makes you strategic.'

'Ponies and people aren't the same,' Edie said impatiently, feeling she was talking to a very small child. 'Listen, Ansti, this whole thing is mental. You seem to think that the fact Mr Robinson's on duty today means we'll get away with it, but he's not as stupid as you think. And Matron will be prowling around too, so she might talk to the taxi driver, even if Mr Robinson doesn't. And if the driver works out that one of his passengers is—'

'Is who?' Anastasia interrupted furiously.

Edie gave an exasperated sigh. It was part of the unreality of Anastasia's life that she never acknowledged she was different. And as for the kidnap – it was never discussed.

'Edie, if you don't want to come that's absolutely fine, but please could you stop being a party pooper. Anyone would think you were on Fothy's side.'

'What do you mean?'

'Don't be so touchy, Edie,' Anastasia said, turning back to the mirror. 'I just wish you wouldn't talk in that boring, responsible voice all the time. You never used to have it, it's as if – oh, for goodness sake, Edie, lighten up!' Anastasia said suddenly. 'It's just a bit of fun. You don't have to come if you don't want to – but there's no need to try and stop the rest of us going. You're not the head girl!'

For a moment Edie imagined staying behind. But what if something went wrong at the fair? Who would Fothy grill for information when Anastasia wasn't back from her so-called *exeat* in time for supper? Edie, of course.

'I'm stuck between a rock and a hard place,' she said with a defeated smile.

'Metaphors!' Anastasia snorted. 'I wasn't listening during that stupid lesson. So what is the difference between a rock and a hard place, clever clogs?'

'There isn't one,' said Edie. 'That was the lesson.'

'So you mean you're not coming?'

'No,' Edie said. 'I mean, I am.'

'The fun starts here!' giggled Belinda, whipping her sketchbook from her bag, and swivelling round in the front seat.

Belinda's skills with a pencil were well known, and the other runaways, squished together in the back, watched in admiration as she made rapid drawings of each of them in turn.

Rose and Anastasia shrieked with delight when they saw their likenesses – Belinda had captured their mood with cartoonish efficiency, drawing them with their fingers pressed to their lips, their eyes sparkling with glee. But Edie had been drawn gulping, with a look of comic fear.

'That's what Edie will look like when we get caught,' Belinda explained, passing her sketchbook to Anastasia for approval. Everyone laughed, and Edie tried to join in, but she felt every bit as anxious as the drawing suggested. Mr Robinson had asked no questions when the taxi had arrived at Knight's Haddon just before lunch, and even Matron, who usually poked her nose into everything, had seemed remarkably incurious when she had happened to wander into the hall as the four girls were writing their names in the *exeat* book. Anastasia had been jubilant about the ease of their escape, but Edie felt unsettled by the lack of interest any of the staff had shown.

'I told you Mr Robinson would be a walkover!' Rose said eagerly, turning to have one last glimpse of the school before the car swung round the bend in the drive. 'He always looks so miserable when he's left in charge – he'd probably be glad if we all ran away!'

'Shhh!' Edie whispered, gesturing meaningfully at the driver – but the others seemed to have forgotten he was there.

'He'll be in no hurry for us to get back,' Anastasia agreed. 'Hey, I've got an idea,' she giggled. 'Let's stay out all night! We could buy a nice painted caravan at the fair!'

Edie looked at her in fright, to be met with a roll of the eyes.

'Oh, Edie, I'm only joking,' Anastasia said, squeezing her arm.

'Yeah, cheer up, Edie, unless you want to look like Belinda's drawing!' Rose laughed.

'Loosen up, Edie . . . Come on, Edie, loosen up . . .' The voices rose in an excited chorus, and as the car slipped out of the school gates into a glare of sunlight Edie tried to shrug off her unease.

'Do you think there'll be hot dogs?' Belinda asked, tearing open a celebratory bag of sweets.

'Oh, there'll be everything dogs,' Rose said dreamily. 'But mainly ponies and horses—'

'Where exactly would you like to be dropped, girls?' interrupted the driver, turning off his music. 'Did you say at the White Horse?'

'No—' Anastasia began, before Rose kicked her silent.

'The White Horse is perfect, thank you,' she said.

The pub car park had already filled up for lunch when the girls were deposited beneath the sign of a rearing white stallion. Edie expected the driver to wait and see them go inside, but he seemed in a hurry to get away.

'Why didn't he ask for any money?' asked Edie, when he had gone.

'Because it just goes on my account, silly,' said Anastasia.

'But it was Rose who ordered the taxi, so how—'

'Oh, please stop worrying about everything,' Anastasia said irritably. 'If you go on like this you'll make me worried too. Can't you just let us enjoy ourselves for a few hours? You've got the rest of the term to play goody two shoes if you want to.'

Edie was annoyed into silence.

The entrance to the fair was a little way down the lane, where crowds of people were flowing into a muddy field, and wading towards a cluster of caravans. Some looked like Romany caravans from story books, wooden and brightly coloured, with smoking chimneys and curved roofs, but most were motor homes, shiny and new.

Rose, alone of the four, had thought to pack a pair of Wellingtons in her rucksack, and looked back in amusement as the others picked their way through the gate, clutching at each other as they tried to hop between the dry patches of grass.

'You might have warned us,' grumbled Anastasia, pulling one of her silver plimsolls from a steaming pile of horse dung.

'It didn't occur to me that you would all be so thick,' Rose replied cheerfully, striding ahead. 'It *is* a horse fair!'

The others followed her across the field, with crowds of people and dogs swarming all around them. A freezing wind was whipping up the hill, and as they got nearer the fair Edie could see rails of clothes and bags of sweets and candyfloss being buffeted about on the stalls.

'Hey, what's he got over there?' Rose said. The others looked where she was pointing, and saw a small, weasel-faced boy standing by a car, his hand rubbing a bulging chest. It was only as they stepped closer that Edie noticed the head of a tiny brown dog peeping from the neck of his hoodie.

'Ooooh!' murmured Belinda, snapping open her sketchbook to capture the scene. Edie lingered in the background while Rose and Anastasia, entranced, raced forward and started firing questions at once.

'It's tiny.'

'It's a Chihuahua,' the boy said proudly.

'Are you selling?'

'Are you shopping?'

'Can I hold?'

'Oh, don't, Ansti, it's too little – you might break it.'

'How old is it?' Anastasia asked.

'Y'mean, how much?' the boy replied, beady.

'No!' Rose said, giving Anastasia a sharp nudge. 'We mean, when were they born?' she asked, glancing pointedly at his jacket, beneath which several other puppies were clearly wriggling.

'Three weeks yesterday.'

'That's too young, they should be with their mother,' Anastasia said censoriously.

'You can be their mam,' said the boy, and promptly whipped the puppy from his own coat and thrust it down Anastasia's, who rewarded him with a screech of pleasure.

'She can have 'im for two,' the boy said to Rose, whom he seemed to have identified as the group's leader.

'Two pounds?' Edie joined in, surprised.

'Two hundred, you fool,' hissed Rose, her eyes warning Edie to keep quiet. 'We're here for the ponies really,' she said, turning back to the boy. 'Thank you for showing us your puppies, and I'm very sorry we can't take one home with us.'

Anastasia, who had extracted the puppy from her coat and was cradling it to her face, let out a wail of protest as Rose prised it from her.

Just then a look of something like fear crossed the face of the Chihuahua-seller and Edie looked up to see a group of four youths approaching, all dressed alike in boots and black capes, and with short mops of brightly-dyed hair. Between them they were carrying bags, and what looked like a folded table. Edie started when she saw them; there was something comic in their appearance – but an air of menace too.

'Oh look,' sniggered Belinda. 'A rainbow gang.'

'Come on,' said Rose, looping arms with Belinda and Anastasia.

Edie glanced back to see the gang of four staring at the boy in silence. 'They're mine to sell if I want to. What business is it of yours, anyway?' said the boy, stuffing the dogs back into his jacket and shuffling uneasily as though he wanted to run away.

Edie clutched Rose's arm. 'Wait!' she whispered, suddenly fearful for the boy.

But then one of the gang threw down his cigarette with a dismissive gesture. 'C'mon, troops,' he said. 'We can't be rescuing puppies and saving the woods at the same time. Let's set up shop.'

And to Edie's relief the group walked away.

'Oh, come on,' Rose said, hurrying them on.

'You are a meanie,' Anastasia protested – then 'Ooh!' she cried, seeing a line of stalls selling pink fur coats and sequinned dresses. Edie lagged behind as the others darted ahead.

A minute later she was startled by an announcement from a loudspeaker: 'Down with the developers! Wildlife threatened by mystery oligarch. Sign here to save Mesmere Wood!'

'Mesmere!' Edie murmured, and turned to see the rainbow gang standing behind a table among the stalls. They were handing out flyers, and a small crowd was gathering. 'Let's go and see,' she whispered to Anastasia, pulling at her sleeve. 'They must be protesting about your father's—'

'Ssh!' Anastasia hissed. 'I don't want to talk about that in front of the others!'

'I'm not going to say anything to them, idiot,' Edie said. 'I just want to find out what they're doing.'

'Shut up! You promised!' Anastasia said irritably. Then, 'Oh, look, how adorable!' she cooed, rushing ahead to join Rose, who was standing by a stall selling caged birds.

I didn't promise not to be curious, Edie thought, but said nothing. The she became aware that she was being stared at by a thin, unshaven man who was sitting at a table beside a hot-dog van. As their eyes locked she felt an eerie sense of familiarity, as if she'd seen him before, and moved away, embarrassed.

'Edie, hurry up! Over here!' Rose called, waving to her through the crowd.

'Them's a breeding pair,' a man was explaining to Belinda, who was busy making a sketch of two tweeting canaries.

'Oh, let's buy them, then they can have babies,' crooned Anastasia, poking a finger through the cage.

'Oh, come on, Anastasia, I want to get to the horses,' Rose said impatiently. 'The auction's starting in ten minutes. You can buy a cart horse if you must.'

Anastasia laughed gleefully, and Belinda hurriedly finished her sketch. But as they were moving on, the man Edie had noticed a few minutes earlier came sloping up to them, trailing plastic bags. Edie was struck by how stooped and dishevelled he looked, and by something pathetic in his smile.

'Hello, girls,' he said, in a low, slightly lurching voice. 'That rucksack you've got on you—'

'Not for sale,' Rose said quickly.

'I never said it was. You must be Knight's Haddon girls. All hail to Knight's Haddon. *Sapere aude!*' the man cried, swinging a bag in the air.

Rose moved on, clearly discomfited, and the others followed.

'That man's weird,' said Anastasia, frowning. 'What do you think he's trying to say?'

'*Sapere aude.* It's our school motto,' Edie replied.

'What does it mean again?'

'Dare to be wise,' Edie said, feeling anything but.

'I wish he'd go away,' said Rose, glancing over her shoulder. 'Would you believe it, he's still following us,' she went on indignantly. 'He's creepy.'

'Not that creepy,' said Belinda. 'Just drunk. Drunk as a skunk.'

'How do you know that?' Edie asked, impressed.

'Couldn't you smell it? He reeked of drink. And he had a bottle peeping out of his pocket – as good as a cartoon.'

'I think we've shaken him off,' Rose said, but then suddenly he reappeared, and thrust a basket into Anastasia's hands.

'They're for Josie,' he said, as he pulled back a filthy scrap of blanket to reveal two thin, furry creatures wriggling about on a bed of straw. 'You give them to Josie, and tell her they're from Stonor. For Josie, from Stonor. Got it?' Then '*Sapere aude,*' he chuckled, before lurching away.

'But . . . hey, wait!' Rose called, but Stonor had gone.

'What are they?' cooed Anastasia, who had lifted one of the animals from the basket and was nuzzling it to her nose in delight.

'Ferrets,' Rose replied. 'My cousins keep them as pets. They're such fun, you can make them climb up your trouser leg and they do a little dance when they get excited.'

'Oooh!' Anastasia squealed.

'Well, they can dance up someone else's trousers, we're not keeping them,' Belinda said firmly. 'Come on, I'll try and catch up with him whoever he was and give them back.' She made to take the basket, but Anastasia pulled it back.

'He won't want them back, he said to give them to Josie,' she said stubbornly.

'But, Anastasia,' Edie said impatiently, 'it must be a mistake. Or a joke.'

'Oh well, it's too late to give them back now,' Anastasia said, smiling slyly. 'You'll never find him.'

Edie looked in the direction the man had gone, but his hat had vanished into the tide of heads.

'What are we going to do?' wailed Rose. 'We can't turn up back at school with two ferrets.'

'Who says we can't?' Anastasia eyes glinted dangerously. 'We'll look after you,' she purred, smiling with pleasure as a ferret wove down her sleeve. 'Come on, let's go and buy them a cashmere blanket!' she went on, tucking the ferrets back into their basket as Belinda and Rose's protests fell on deaf ears.

'Where will you keep them?' Rose asked practically.

'In the animal house, of course,' Anastasia said.

Belinda rolled her eyes. The animal house was a narrow green shed hidden behind the tennis courts, where pet hamsters, rabbits and guinea pigs were allowed to board during the school term. Mrs Prentice, the new art mistress, was in charge of it, and there was often a waiting list for places. Girls had to wait until they reached the second year before their pets were even considered for admission.

'There's no room,' Belinda said.

'Yes, there is,' Anastasia said. 'Phoebe's rabbit died of flu over Christmas.'

'I thought it died of over-eating,' Rose said.

'Whatever, but the point is it's dead, so now there's a spare cage. We can sneak them in there after supper.'

'But what will Mrs Prentice say?' Rose asked.

'Nothing,' Anastasia said firmly. 'You know what the

Prent's like. She never notices anything.'

'Don't be daft, the Prent knows every animal by name,' Belinda said. 'Phoebe's heard her talking to them. Of course she'll notice if a couple of ferrets suddenly appear!'

The others agreed. There had never been ferrets in the animal house before.

'Well, she'll get a lovely surprise – won't she, my little darlings,' Anastasia purred, cooing into the basket. 'Prenty and I will look after you, and we'll feed you all the most delicious things. You are *beautiful*. I shall call you Precious and Treasure, yes, Precious and Treasure, because that is what you are to me.'

'Oh, do see sense, Ansti,' Rose said sharply. 'When the Prent finds them she's bound to tell Fothy!'

'And Fothy's bound to send them back,' Edie pointed out.

'No she won't,' Anastasia said defiantly, hugging the basket to her chest. 'I won't allow it.'

Edie knew better than to try and reason with Anastasia when she was in a mood like this. She would have to find something more exciting to distract her – only then might Anastasia be persuaded to give up the ferrets.

But distraction came sooner than they expected.

'Hello, girls,' came a calm voice which filled everyone with dread – and they turned to see Miss Fotheringay greeting them with thunder in her eyes.

Pets Keep Pets

Miss Fotheringay said nothing as she herded her quarry through the crowds towards the car park. The atmosphere at the fair was at carnival pitch. A fiddler had struck up beside the bonfire, and there were children dancing with dogs yapping at their heels – but the headmistress's ill humour seemed to embrace everyone. When the birdman sprang out in front of them jangling a cage of miniature parrots, she saw him off with a furious look.

Edie was glad at least that she appeared not to have noticed the wicker basket that Anastasia was dangling furtively by her knees, the ferrets hidden only by the thin scrap of blanket she had tucked over them. Edie glanced at it apprehensively, praying they wouldn't squeal.

'Wait here,' Miss Fotheringay said tersely when they reached the car park. She turned and waved at someone, and next moment Edie saw the colourful figure of Mrs Prentice weaving towards them. Mrs Prentice was famous for her theatrical clothes and had dressed for the fair in a drooping velvet skirt and bright orange Wellingtons, with her red hair tumbling down her back like a mermaid.

'There you girls are! There are so many people, I was afraid for a moment that we might have lost you!' she said, seemingly unaware of the trouble they were in.

'Anastasia, you can come with me. The rest of you can go back with Mrs Prentice,' Miss Fotheringay said, signalling them through the gate.

Anastasia's face fell.

'They must have followed us,' Rose whispered, as Miss Fotheringay led them across the car park. 'How else could they have known we were here? We never told anyone.'

'Except Phoebe,' Anastasia said darkly.

'Phoebe won't have told. I know she's spiteful but she understands the rules.'

'Anastasia, quick! Give them to me!' Rose whispered, quickly snatching the basket of ferrets before they reached the mistress's cars.

'Belinda, dear, why don't you come in the front?' the Prent said, with a warm smile at her favourite.

Rose – with Edie's help – smuggled the basket of ferrets on to the floor of the back seat without the Prent seeming to notice.

As the car bumped out of the field over the cattle grid one of the ferrets let out a squeal, but the art mistress appeared oblivious.

It was curious, Edie thought, clutching the basket between her feet, the way the Prent talked about being 'always alert to the world around you' while never detecting mischief under her nose.

'I'm very glad we found you,' Mrs Prentice said, fishing a packet of humbugs from the glove locker, and passing them round. 'Miss Fotheringay was in a terrible state when I bumped into her. She said she'd seen you all go in, but then lost you in the crowd – anyone would think you were in danger of being spirited away by goblins, the worry she was in! I was surprised to see her there, I wouldn't have thought it was her sort of thing – but oh, I do love the horse fair. I've been going for years. Did you get some good pictures, Belinda?'

Belinda produced her sketchbook, and she and Rose chatted with Mrs Prentice, but Edie sat in silence, wondering what was going on in the other car.

It was still daylight when they arrived back at Knight's Haddon. The whole adventure, Edie noted, had lasted less than two hours.

'I hope you won't have missed tea,' the Prent said, smiling, as they clambered out, furtively clutching the basket.

The other car had not returned, so as soon as Mrs Prentice had driven away the girls fled behind the tennis courts and held a tense consultation.

'We should come clean with the Prent and ask if she can find room for them in the animal house and make her promise not to tell Fothy. She's such a sport, I bet she'll agree,' Belinda said.

'She wouldn't dare!' Edie protested. 'Fothy would go mad if she found out.'

'And she'll go mad if we tell her,' Rose said nervously.

'Well, we're going to have to tell someone,' said Belinda, and one of the ferrets let out a squeal of agreement.

The next moment they saw Miss Fotheringay's car appearing down the drive.

'Let's hide them in here, then we can come back and feed them later,' Belinda said, hurriedly snaffling the basket into the little wooden lean-to where the tennis balls were stored. 'Anastasia will know what they like to eat.'

Edie smiled grimly, suspecting that Anastasia knew as little about ferrets as she did.

The girls trooped inside, dreading their encounter with the headmistress. But tea time came and went and still there was no summons to the headmistress's study. Anastasia, meanwhile, did not reappear. Edie and Rose slunk back to the shed to feed the ferrets some bread they had smuggled out of the dining room, and afterwards the three girls sat huddled guiltily in the common room – though it was clear the other second years knew nothing of the trouble they were in.

'Perhaps Anastasia's been sent home!' Rose said.

'If she's been sent home, then we will be too!' Belinda whispered.

Edie felt sick at the prospect of a forced return to Folly Farm, then put the thought away as unlikely to happen. Fothy would find a way of protecting her from that, she thought guiltily.

It was not until after supper that Matron finally came and singled them out – and to their surprise it was Miss Mannering, not the headmistress, to whom they were told to report.

'Well, girls, what have you got to say for yourselves?' Miss Mannering said, looking at the culprits crossly over her spectacles. She was sitting at her desk, the floor around her strewn with timetables and piles of marking. 'I am, as you can see, quite busy.'

'We're very sorry,' said Edie. 'We know it was a stupid thing to do.'

'Of course you do,' Miss Mannering replied. 'You're not stupid, any of you, therefore it stands to reason that you know when you have been. You have to think about Anastasia. It's boring for you, but there it is – she is a kidnap risk. Edith has reason to know this better than anyone. The school's policy is not to speak of it, but to assume that you are all sufficiently mature to know that everyone has to be extra careful around her. What you have done today has made the need for outside security at the school that much more likely. Which both Miss Fotheringay and I think would be a very great pity. Did any strangers approach you at the fair?'

'No,' Rose said quickly. 'We were hardly there any time at all. But—'

'Yes?' said the Man.

'Where – where is Anastasia?' Rose asked timidly.

'She is spending the day in the sick room,' Miss Mannering replied, 'to give her time to contemplate the folly of her ways.'

The girls were bewildered as to how lightly they had got off. So much for being sent home – they had only been gated for one weekend!

'The Man must be going soft,' Rose said, skipping down the corridor.

'Fothy must have told her not to be too hard on us,' Belinda mused. 'I suppose she didn't want Edie to get in too much trouble, so we've all been spared!' She seemed delighted, clearly thinking that Edie's special relationship with Miss Fotheringay had worked in everyone's favour.

But Edie squirmed. And if Miss Fotheringay was feeling so lenient, then why was she keeping Anastasia in solitary confinement?

When Anastasia finally reappeared at bedtime, her expression was distraught.

'What happened to you lot?' she demanded, storming into the dormitory and flinging herself on her bed.

Belinda and Rose told her, and Anastasia let out an outraged howl. 'That's so unfair. I've been gated for the whole term, and . . . and – I'm going to have to stay at school for the *exeat* weekend! Fothy was foul. In the car she didn't speak except to say, "I will call your father, Anastasia, and ask him what to do." And when we got back to school she made me stand next to her desk while she rang him. "What action do you advise, Prince? I see. Oh yes, that should not be too difficult to arrange." Oh, you should have heard her! She was enjoying it!'

'What did your father say?' Edie asked.

'He told her to make me sorry!' Anastasia said furiously. 'I could hear him down the phone, his voice was so cold, like he was talking about some minion on his staff. "*I look to you, Miss Fotheringay, to make sure it never happens again.*" She asked him if he wanted to talk to me, but he said he couldn't trust himself because he was so angry. And it's my birthday!' she sobbed. 'The worst birthday of my life! Papa *hates* me.'

'He doesn't hate you, Anastasia,' Edie said, trying to calm her. 'It's only because—'

'Oh, I know!' Anastasia interrupted her, her voice shaking. 'It's only because he's so worried that . . . that something will happen again! And you're worried too, aren't you, Edie?' she went on savagely. 'That's why you told Fothy to follow us!'

'What?' Edie had been sitting on the end of Anastasia's bed, but now she stood up, as if she had been kicked.

'Oh, dear, has little Edie been a tell-tale tit?' sniped Phoebe, spitting a mouthful of toothpaste into the sink.

But Edie hardly heard. She was staring at Anastasia, willing her to retract.

Anastasia looked back, defiant. 'Fothy gave your game away, Edie. She told me she'd had to miss lunch with her father to follow us – well, you'd know all about that, because she asked you to go too!'

'What do you mean?' Edie whispered, aghast.

'You know perfectly well what I mean! And that's why Fothy's let you off so lightly – as a reward for shopping me!'

'What are you saying, Ansti?' Belinda said. 'What did Fothy say exactly?' Belinda's voice was level, but Edie bristled at the way she looked only at Anastasia, not at her.

'She let it slip,' Anastasia spat. '"*I was going to take Edith home for lunch!*" she said. 'Huh!'

'Is it true, Edie?' Rose asked, puzzled. 'Did Fothy ask you home for lunch?'

'Y–yes,' Edie said, feeling her face burn. 'But I didn't tell her! I swear on my life!'

'But, Edie, why didn't you tell us Fothy had asked you to go home with her?' Belinda said.

'What's it matter?' Edie snapped. 'All I said was that I couldn't go because I was having lunch with Anastasia—'

'At the fair!' Anastasia cut in mockingly.

'Don't be mad – of course I didn't say that!' Edie cried.

'Temper tantrum,' Phoebe said snidely. 'Settle it with a pillow fight, always best.'

'Shut up!' Edie hissed.

'Oh, come on, we're all in enough trouble as it is, let's not make it worse by falling out,' Rose appealed. 'And let's not forget the ferrets.'

'The ferrets!' Belinda gulped. 'Oh, Ansti, we hid them in the tennis shed!'

'Edie can look after them – they're her ferrets now,' Anastasia said.

'What do you mean?' Edie asked.

'Oh, come on,' Anastasia said, tugging off her jersey, and tossing it on the bed. 'We all know you're Fothy's pet. If I tell her they're my ferrets she'll send them straight back to the fair – but if you say they're your ferrets, Edie, she'll give them a VIP cage. *Edith's ferrets, oh well, we'll have to take extra special care of them and feed them roast beef and caramel squares,*' Anastasia said mockingly. 'The animal house won't be good enough for them if she thinks they're your ferrets. She'll probably take them to live with her in the West Tower! She'll keep them in her bedroom, and knit them scarves!'

Edie looked at her in contempt, but Belinda and Rose seemed to rise to Anastasia's idea.

'That's brilliant thinking, Ansti – Fothy's much more likely to let us keep them if she thinks they're Edie's,' Belinda said excitedly.

'Only pets are allowed to keep pets,' said Rose, smiling. 'Is that a pun or a metaphor?'

'I think you should go and talk to her tonight,' Belinda urged. 'The sooner we come clean the better. Don't say anything about that weird man, just tell her that you won them at a coconut shy or something.'

Edie felt the tears stinging her eyes. They all thought she had betrayed them! Edie knew Miss Fotheringay would be furious when she owned up about the ferrets, but at least it would prove she wasn't the headmistress's pet.

'All right, I'll go and take the flak,' she said boldly. 'But I warn you, when I tell her they're mine she'll probably shoot them!'

Wrong-Footed!

'Well, Edith?'

Edie had been expecting a riot act, but there was no anger in the face that looked up at her from behind the desk on the far side of the study.

Anastasia's accusations were still ringing in her ears, and as she was steered to the sofa she felt her courage failing. She was aware of Miss Fotheringay lowering herself on to the sofa beside her, holding Black Puss, and of the dull red light of the fire dancing through a haze of tears.

'Tell me what's happened, Edith,' Miss Fotheringay said quietly, stroking Black Puss, who lay purring loudly in her lap. 'I can't help you if you keep secrets from me.'

'I'm sorry,' Edie mumbled, wiping her eyes with her sleeve. 'I'm sorry about – about the fair.'

'We have dealt with that,' Miss Fotheringay said gently. 'Or at least Miss Mannering has. I have no more to say on the matter.'

'But Anastasia said that you—'

'Anastasia, I have no doubt, has told you that I am a witch, and many more unpleasant things besides,' Miss Fotheringay said, smiling. 'She may feel that she has been dealt with harshly, but she has done a very foolish thing and now she is paying the price.'

'But it wasn't just Anastasia,' Edie protested. 'It was all of us. We were all in it together, and we agreed that if we got caught we'd all take the blame.'

'And you *have* all taken the blame,' Miss Fotheringay replied firmly. 'You seem to forget, Edith, that you have all been gated next weekend – this means that once again I will not be able to take you to see my father.' She raised her hands in a gesture of defeat. 'Yes,' she said, seeing Edie's crestfallen face. 'In a sense, Edith, you have punished us both by your misguided little escapade. And if I have come down slightly harder on Anastasia, that is because she of all of you should have best understood the potential consequences to her safety. Anastasia is thirteen now and there is a limit to the special allowances we can make for her.'

The headmistress paused, and looked at Edie probingly. Edie knew she was trying to find out what, if anything, she knew about the prince's plans for the tower.

'She is certainly old enough to take some small level of responsibility for her behaviour – and certainly too old to be sending you scuttling to my office before bedtime to try and get me to soften my stance.'

Edie wondered if she dared to mention the ferrets after all, but when Miss Fotheringay spoke again her tone was different.

'Now, Edith, I want to know about you. What's happened, dear child? Who's made you cry?'

A part of Edie longed to confide in her that Anastasia was being horrid. But instead she lurched into the subject of the ferrets. This at least was a tale that Anastasia had instructed her to tell.

'So you see we – I – ended up with some ferrets – two, a pair, we think they're two girls . . . Rose had a look, but it was basically quite hard to tell, and anyway, we – I – brought them back to school. In – in a basket,' Edie finished clumsily.

Edie knew Miss Fotheringay would be furious, and she hardly dared to meet her eye. But a part of her looked forward to being punished – then at least Anastasia would have to believe she wasn't the headmistress's pet. And Edie didn't care if Miss Fotheringay refused her permission to keep the ferrets in the animal house. Secretly she didn't like them. She thought they were sly and evil-looking – like her cousin Lyle.

Miss Fotheringay sat very still, her face betraying none of the rage that Edie expected. 'You say you brought them back to school?'

Edie nodded.

'But tell me, child, where are they now?' Miss Fotheringay's eyes roved about Edie's person, as if expecting that one of the creatures might suddenly peek out.

'We – I . . . hid them in the tennis ball shed – but Ana— I . . . wanted to ask if I could keep them in the animal house,' Edie stammered.

'I see,' Miss Fotheringay said slowly. She sat silently a moment, then replaced her spectacles on her nose, as if to see the situation more clearly. 'So,' she concluded, 'Anastasia rushed off and spent her pocket money on two ferrets, and now she doesn't know what to do with them and calculating – not unreasonably – that she is in quite enough trouble as it is, she has decided that the ferrets might as well belong to you.'

'No!' Edie cried, shaken that her story should have been so easily seen through. 'It wasn't like that. They're not really any of ours—'

'Not really yours?' Miss Fotheringay arched an eyebrow. 'Did you steal them, Edith?'

'No!' Edie bit her lip. Rose had told the Man that they hadn't spoken to any strangers.

'We – we bought them,' she said.

'We?' queried Miss Fotheringay.

Edie squirmed. *She knows I'm lying*, she thought, *but not where the lie lies*.

'Well,' said the headmistress, at length, 'have you nothing more to say?'

'I . . . we – need to know what to do about them,' Edie replied desperately.

'Ah, yes, what to do about them,' Miss Fotheringay said, looking at Edie with a hint of challenge. 'Well, Edith, what do you think? Do you want to keep the poor creatures locked up for ever in a cage, scrabbling about in circles, denied their liberty? Denied even the chance to breed . . . if we are to trust Rose's diagnosis of their sexes. Or shall we tiptoe out to the tennis courts now, Edith, you and me, and let the wretched creatures go while no one's looking? We can set them down in the park, and watch them scamper away by moonlight, up the hill, into the beech wood, and on and on, out of sight, into the vast beyond, free at last, Edith, free at last!'

Miss Fotheringay's voice rose to a trembling pitch, and she turned to Edie with her fist clenched in the air – then collapsed in laughter when she saw her pupil's startled expression.

'It's all right, Edith, you may keep your ferrets in the animal house if you must. I shall tell Mrs Prentice to expect them. Let me know what they like to eat,' she added smiling, 'and I can order in some supplies.'

One Thing and Another

Edie did not go back to Anastasia's dormitory that night. She had scored a victory in ensuring the ferrets could stay at school – but she knew Anastasia would take it as another sign of Miss Fotheringay's favouritism.

'Where did you get to today?' asked Janet as Edie was getting into bed. 'There was a terrible atmosphere. Someone said you'd run away!'

'We went to a horse fair,' Edie replied flatly. 'It was stupid.'

'Stupid? Why?'

'Because we got caught, and now we're in trouble.'

'Doesn't sound stupid to me,' Janet said enviously. 'I wish I could have come.'

'I'm sorry,' Edie said hastily. 'It was Anastasia's

birthday and we took a taxi and there wouldn't of been room.'

'You mean that the idea of asking me didn't even come up?'

Edie looked sheepish.

'I don't care anyway.' Janet shrugged. 'Anastasia hates me. She's probably got a point.'

'No, she hasn't!' Edie said fiercely – then stopped, realizing she'd confirmed Janet's hunch. Then, 'Hey, do you like ferrets?' she asked, changing the subject.

'Ferrets?'

'We got some at the fair.'

Janet looked interested. 'Where are they now?'

Edie explained anxiously about the basket in the tennis ball shed, its lid held down by a stone. 'Fothy said I could put them in the animal house tomorrow, but she didn't say anything about tonight. Do you think they'll freeze to death?'

Janet looked at her slyly. 'Would you care if they did?'

'They give me the creeps,' Edie admitted. 'And they stink. But I've got to look after them. They're Ansti's, you see – I mean, she was the one that wanted to keep them, but . . .' Edie floundered. 'Oh, you know what she's like. She won't know what they need.'

Janet snorted. 'I see. So now you're Ansti's ferret-keeper and you're terrified that the royal pets will pick up a cold, or else—' She raised her hand, as if firing a gun: 'Pow! Princess Anastasia extracts a blood-filled revenge!' Then, 'Oh, don't look so worried, Edie,' she said, laughing. 'They'll be fine. I'll help you sort them out tomorrow.'

The next morning Janet took charge. On Sundays the girls were allowed a lie-in, with breakfast being served until nine, but Janet shook Edie awake early, and hurried her down to the dining room before the other second years had got out of bed. The tables were mostly empty, with only Matron and a few sixth-formers among the early risers.

'Smuggle out some bacon,' she whispered to Edie, folding a rasher inside a slice of bread, and tucking it into her pocket. 'In fact,' she said, grabbing a handful of sugar lumps, 'smuggle out anything you can.'

Edie was just going up to the counter for a second helping when Anastasia appeared behind her. She seldom made it down to breakfast before nine o'clock on Sundays, and Edie could tell from her swollen face that she had been crying. Something in her appearance made Edie's anger vanish. 'Ansti, listen,' she began excitedly, suddenly eager to share the good news, 'Fothy's said we can keep the ferrets in the animal house and Janet says she'll help us. She knows what to feed them.'

But Anastasia silenced her with a withering look: 'I told you Fothy'd let you keep them! She'd do anything for you!'

'But – what, what do you mean? We all know they're yours, Anastasia.'

'Did you tell Fothy they were mine?' Anastasia asked accusingly.

'No, of course not. I – I didn't want to get you into

trouble.'

'Well, she must have guessed, otherwise why would she have done something so mean?'

'What?' Edie asked, baffled.

'Said I can't go to the animal house!' Anastasia spat. 'She just told me, just now! "Ah, Anastasia, there you are! Edie tells me you've all brought some ferrets back to school. But I'm afraid you won't be able to visit them – I'm sorry, my dear, but you're not allowed to visit the animal house while you're gated."'

Edie looked crestfallen. 'But that's so unfair. Why would she do that?'

'Because she hates me, that's why!' said Anastasia, before taking herself off to an empty table.

'Did I just see what I think I saw?' asked Janet, as Edie returned, dejected, to her place.

'What do you mean?'

'That your Russian princess just gave you a right royal telling-off.'

'Oh, shut up,' Edie returned. But in truth she found Janet's teasing easier than Anastasia's storms.

The other second years were still arriving in the dining room when Edie and Janet cleared their plates and slipped outside.

'This way,' Edie smiled, as Janet made off in the wrong direction. It was one of the many surprising things about Janet that despite being so clever in class she seemed incapable of mastering the basic layout of the school. Even a simple trip from the East Tower to the North Tower could still result in her getting lost.

'You shouldn't laugh,' Janet said, following Edie past the kitchens and out across the drive. 'You wouldn't laugh if I was blind, or deaf, so you shouldn't laugh at my having no sense of direction. It's just as much of a disability.'

'No, it's not,' Edie said, thinking of Babka, her Polish grandmother, who was blind. 'Now, look, Thicko, that's the tennis ball shed over there.' She pointed across the row of sodden grass courts, with their faded white markings, their nets lowered for the winter. When they got closer she saw that the door of the shed was swinging open, and felt a surge of panic, imagining a fox creeping in by night. She broke into a run, dreading what she'd find – but the basket was still there.

Janet reached it down from the shelf and pulled back the cloth.

'They're dead!' Edie shrieked, looking in horror at the two corpses spread rigid on the straw.

'No they're not, idiot,' Janet said, rousing the two ferrets to life with a poke. She seemed to know exactly what to do. She swung the basket over her arm, and when they reached the animal house she tipped the ferrets out on to the floor and started tossing them bits of bacon.

'Careful – they might run away!' Edie said, but the ferrets showed no interest in the open door, and went on prancing after their breakfast.

'Aren't they funny?' said Janet. 'What shall we call them?'

'Precious and Treasure,' Edie said. 'That's what

Anastasia called them.'

Janet wrinkled her nose, her glasses nearly falling off as she did so. 'Yuk! I don't like those. I think we should call them Thing One and Thing Two, from *The Cat in the Hat*. Much better!'

'You can't change their names,' Edie protested.

But Janet's mind was set. 'Thing One, Thing Two, Thing Two, Thing One,' she chanted, dancing a wild dervish around the ferrets as she splashed water over their heads in an ad-hoc christening ceremony.

Edie found Janet's attitude to the ferrets refreshing. She'd hated the way Anastasia had wanted her to coo over them and nuzzle them to her nose, but so long as they were just wriggling about on the floor she didn't find them nearly so revolting.

'Precious and Treasure!' Janet scoffed. 'What ridiculous names! Stand up and rejoice, ye ferrets of the horse fair, from now on you shall live in dignity as Thing One and Thing Two.'

Edie laughed – but then she became aware of a figure in the doorway, and saw Anastasia looking on in horror. 'Anastasia!' she exclaimed stupidly.

'What are you doing with them?' Anastasia demanded. 'You can't call them Things! They're my ferrets, *mine* – and I called them Precious and Treasure! What do you think you're doing, stealing them and – and changing their names!'

Edie winced. Couldn't Anastasia hear how idiotic she sounded? 'Janet said she'd help me look after them, that's all,' she said. 'And you're not allowed up here,

Ansti. You'd better not let Fothy find you.'

'Fothy!' Anastasia snorted. 'Sorry. I'd forgotten you were her henchman!'

Janet sucked in her breath. 'Steady! From what I heard, you're the one who asked Edie to take the rap for bringing the ferrets back to school. And your ploy was successful, insofar as Fothy has agreed to spare their necks.'

'Of course she has!' said Anastasia with an accusing look at Edie.

'However, the headmistress's mercy,' Janet continued grandly, holding up her hand for silence, 'led to another problem. Edie, you see, doesn't like ferrets, and doesn't know what to do with them. So Muggins here said she'd help out. Which is what I'm doing. And now, where are we going to put them?'

Edie pointed to the empty cage on the bottom shelf that used to house Phoebe's rabbit. But when they inspected it they found the door swinging half-broken from its hinges.

'We'll have to repair it,' Janet said efficiently. 'I'll need nails and a hammer for starters.'

But before the operation could begin, Belinda and Rose appeared.

Anastasia nodded at them, and Edie saw something conspiratorial in their expressions.

'Not so fast,' Anastasia said, facing Edie with her arms crossed. 'We want to know something. How did Fothy find out about the fair?'

Edie looked at her, dumbfounded. Surely she couldn't

be bringing this up again.

'You have to admit that it does look like you,' Anastasia said slowly. 'But of course, if you say it wasn't you, then I owe you an apology.'

'I accept your apology,' Edie said coolly – but Anastasia was in full stride.

'Perhaps it was Janet who accidentally-on-purpose let something slip.'

'Don't be so stupid!' Janet said crossly. 'How could I have snitched on you when I didn't even know that you were planning a bunk-out? You didn't invite me – remember?'

'So where were you yesterday morning? After breakfast we all came back to the dormitories but you weren't there.'

'What are you suggesting?' said Janet.

Anastasia looked at her darkly. 'That you took up a spying position somewhere, and then told someone what you'd seen.'

'And why would I have done that?'

'You're a new bug,' said Rose half-apologetically. 'You might not know about Not Telling.'

Janet threw a look of contempt at all of them. 'Of course I know. I have been to school before. Can't you do better than blaming the new girl when anything goes wrong?'

'Don't get so rattled, Janet. We're just trying to work out what happened. Edie, what do you think?'

'I think Fothy isn't stupid, but the plan was!' Edie said, before she could stop herself.

'Good point well made,' said Janet, with a laconic smile. 'Now, is anyone going to find me a hammer?'

'Ansti – wait!' Edie cried, as Anastasia turned and left, slamming the door behind her.

Edie would never have dreamed that two ferrets could cause so much fuss. She was officially in charge of them, but during the two weeks that followed she found herself caught up in a simmering custody battle between Janet and Anastasia, both of whom seemed to think the miserable little creatures were their own. Edie was both amused and alarmed as the two girls competed for the ferrets' favour, smuggling them tasty tidbits from the dining room, and giving them socks and loo rolls to tunnel in inside their cage.

One morning, just over a week after the ferrets had arrived, Edie found Janet in the animal house, triumphant, having made them a hammock out of a pair of gym knickers. But when Anastasia discovered it at lunch time, she took it down.

'Precious and Treasure don't sleep in people's pants,' she said to Edie, fiercely.

The fact that the animal house remained out of bounds for Anastasia did nothing to hold her back. If anything, she seemed to feel that the clandestine nature of her visits made her affection even stronger.

'It's easy enough for Janet,' she said to Edie dismissively. 'She can visit them whenever she likes. But I have to take risks.'

Anastasia had in place a cunning plan of setting off

after lunch in the direction of the music rooms, purposefully swinging her violin, then slipping outside unseen through one of the practice-room windows. But in the evenings the music rooms were locked and it was harder to escape.

Then it was left to Edie to feed the ferrets, while Anastasia sat moping in the common room.

'Poor darlings, were they missing me?' Anastasia wailed on the Wednesday evening, when Edie came back.

'Pining!' Edie joked.

Anastasia looked mollified. Then her face darkened: 'Was Janet there?' Then, 'Oh, why can't she just leave them alone?' she said irritably, when Edie's silence confirmed her fears.

Edie looked weary. She was glad that Anastasia hadn't been there to see what a fuss Janet had been making of Thing One and Thing Two, as she continued to call them, teaching them tricks and setting them down to race.

'Edie!' Anastasia said suddenly, looking at her with burning eyes. 'Have you made it absolutely clear to Janet that my Precious and Treasure are not up for adoption?'

'I think she knows that,' Edie replied, smiling.

'It's not funny, Edie! Imagine what it feels like when you all sneak off there in the evening to canoodle with my pets!'

Edie sighed. 'I've told you before, Ansti, I never canoodle the blasted creatures!'

'Don't call Precious and Treasure blasted!' said

Anastasia, with a tell-tale tremble of her lip.

'Well, at least we're not fighting for their affection,' Edie said, trying to humour her.

Anastasia smiled feebly. 'Oh, Edie,' she said plaintively, 'promise me you won't let Janet get too close to them!'

But Janet's enthusiasm for the ferrets showed no sign of waning. Every night, when Edie went to feed them, Janet was there. And on Friday night Edie found Belinda and Rose in attendance too, squealing with delight as they watched Janet race the ferrets across the floor.

Edie stood on the outside of the circle, trying to imagine what would happen when Anastasia's gating was lifted. Would Treasure be torn in two like a Christmas cracker, with Newgirl pulling one end and Anastasia another?

'The thing about ferrets,' said Janet, 'is that they're as loyal as dogs and as playful as monkeys – and did you know that their coats change colour in summer from white to brown?'

'How come you know so much about them?'

'Because my father used to have some.'

'I love them changing colour,' said Belinda. 'I'm going to draw a picture of the change-over.'

Thing One and Thing Two meanwhile, perhaps guessing that their free time had a clock on it, took advantage of the girls' chatter to disappear. Janet eventually found them curled up behind a cage of guinea pigs, and seized them both in one swoop.

She tenderly slipped Thing One into the hutch, while

Thing Two she cradled briefly in her right arm, her left hand resting lightly on its neck.

'They're one of the oldest pets,' she said, and described a painting she'd seen in which a woman was holding one.

'I know that picture,' said Belinda thoughtfully. 'Do you remember, Rose? The Prent showed it to us last term.'

Rose looked blank.

'You must remember!' said Belinda. 'It was by the mystery smiling woman man. The Mona is-it-a-smile-or-is-it-a-scowl Lisa. You know, by Leonardo da Someone. You can't have forgotten that as well!'

Edie smiled, thinking how impressed Babka would be by Belinda's memory for anything visual.

'You've lost me, Belinda,' said Rose. 'I don't know what I'm trying to remember. Man ferret woman mystery smile scowl.'

'You're hopeless,' said Belinda, clutching her pen. 'Anyway, I'm going to have a crack at drawing Anastasia in the same pose as in the picture by the Mona Lisa man – one of the world's best artists *ever* to you ignoramuses! Then maybe next year we can go to the fair again and present it to the ferret man. He might even pay me for it.'

'The man you bought them off?' asked Janet. 'How much did he charge? I'd like to buy another one, and start a ferret dynasty.'

'Start away – he didn't charge anything!' Rose said. 'He gave them to us as a present.'

'A present?' Janet looked impressed.

'Rose thought he was drunk – but I thought he was just kind,' Belinda said.

'You can be kind and drunk,' said Rose with a shrug. 'I have a brother who's often both.'

'Drunk or not, he was certainly muddled,' Edie joined in. 'He said the ferrets were for Josie – well, we knew there wasn't a Josie at Knight's Haddon but he seemed pretty set on the idea.'

The lighting was dim in the animal house and none of the girls noticed that the colour had drained from Janet's face. 'What did the ferret man look like?' she asked quietly.

'Like this,' said Belinda, opening her sketchbook with an air of triumphant flourish.

8

KNIGHT'S HADDON

Mischief at Midnight

It was just on midnight when the small casement window in the cloakroom creaked open, and a girlish figure slipped out from the pitch interior, and dropped silently into the flowerbed. It had been raining earlier in the night, but now the air was cool and clear, and the moon was floating above the low crest of woods beyond the park, showing the pale silvery outline of the tree-tops. The child stood still, crouched animal-like against the wall, her head hidden inside the hood of a dressing gown. Everything was very quiet and still, the only sound the faint murmur of a car passing on the lane towards the village, but the child remained frozen, peering into the darkness as if in fear. Then finally she pulled a torch from the pocket of her dressing gown, and ran nimbly across the drive, and up along the steep, winding path towards the tennis courts.

When she reached the animal house beyond the netting of the furthest court she turned a moment and looked back towards the school, at the four black towers that rose inkily into the moonlit sky. Then she unbolted the shed door and vanished inside. Her torchlight could be seen flickering behind the half-open door, but when she emerged a moment later the torch was extinguished, and she was clutching to her stomach a wire cage. She stumbled a little way across the lawn, then knelt down on the ground with the cage in front of her, and leant over it, fumbling clumsily with the door. Finally it opened and she stood back and watched silently as two ferrets slithered out on to the grass and stood tentatively sniffing the air.

The girl clapped her hands, softly at first, and hissed encouragement, 'Go on, shoo!'

The ferrets scampered on a few paces, each veering in a different direction, but then stopped, as if confused by the unaccustomed vastness of the lawn. A moment later they took off again, but only to double back and cavort in circles around the cage.

The girl clapped again, louder this time, and rushed at them as if in a sudden rage, her voice rising to a cry: 'Run! Go! Go on, you idiots, run! You're free!'

The ferrets froze, startled, then they took off, their bodies twisting and looping through the long grass, prancing in a sudden frenzy of glee, up the bank, into the tangled thicket, on and on, faster and faster, towards the hills and the woods, and the silent call of the wild.

As the hooded figure fled back across the lawn a light came on at the top of the West Tower. An instant later the curtains drew apart and the headmistress appeared at the open window and stood peering down across the park. She heard the clattering of wings and saw a bird rise in fright from the trees, then a cloud slipped over the moon and the night turned black.

Eustacia Stone and the Helicopter Dash

'I wish you weren't still gated,' said Edie to Anastasia on the third Saturday of term. 'It's a lovely afternoon to walk into the village.'

Anastasia, who was always cold, was sitting by the radiator in the common room, hunched over a book.

'Is it?' she said in a depressed voice, gazing vacantly out of the window. 'Looks a bit frosty to me.'

'That's just the point,' Edie said. 'A beautiful frosty winter's day.'

Anastasia gave a dramatic shudder. 'Call me spoilt but I prefer real cold, as in Russia, or real sun – as in the South of France.'

'I do call you spoilt,' Edie smiled.

'And I call you horrid,' Anastasia said. 'I can't help

being spoilt, just like you can't help being Fothy's favourite.'

Edie was hurt. She depended on Anastasia understanding her special relationship with the headmistress – the others could tease all they liked, but Ansti was her friend and ally.

Or had been. For now whenever she mentioned Miss Fotheringay to Edie, it was in a goading tone.

'Oh, go to the village, why don't you?' Anastasia said. 'You can buy some toys for Precious and Treasure.'

'There's no point, they'll only eat them,' Edie replied dismissively.

'Don't speak about them like that!'

Edie looked at her in exasperation. 'Oh, come on, Ansti. You know I'm happy to look after your ferrets for you, but I've never pretended to like them! I hate the way they wriggle and scratch and look straight through me with their weird lidless eyes.' She shuddered. 'They remind me of Lyle.'

'They are not like Lyle!'

'How do you know?' Edie laughed. 'You've never met him!'

Anastasia looked furious. 'Please don't feel you have to look after my ferrets any more, then. In fact, I forbid you to go anywhere near them.'

'You can't order me around!' said Edie. 'I'm not your servant, Anastasia. I'll do exactly what I like.'

'Of course you will,' said Anastasia. 'You always have.'

Edie looked at her coldly. 'Is that really what you think? Because don't you know that what I'd really like to do is to let your ferrets go free?'

'Go away!' shouted Anastasia. 'Go away and stay away from my ferrets. Yes! It's an order!'

Edie was shaking. But Anastasia made no sign of making amends as she picked up her book with a stony face.

In the dormitory Sally and Alice were preparing for a trip to the village, and Edie was relieved when they asked her to join them.

She said nothing of the scene with Anastasia, and soon found herself affected by Sally and Alice's good humour. As they reached the village Edie felt a guilty rush of pleasure: just because Anastasia was in a rage, it didn't mean that Edie had to be miserable too.

As they were heading back to school they met Belinda and Rose, and they all linked arms and marched along together, swinging their bags of shopping in a sudden surge of high spirits.

Edie looked around her, taking pleasure in the frozen stillness of the landscape, only half listening as the others began to complain about the short cut through the woods now being out of bounds.

'What I don't understand is will they ever be *in* bounds again?' asked Sally. 'Or has the person who's bought the tower bought the woods too?'

'I think so,' said Rose. 'And now they're going to chop down lots of trees to make some stupid garden. *And* a new road to get to the tower. That's why those people wanted everyone to sign their petition at the horse fair.'

'I wish you'd invited me to the fair!' Sally said. 'It sounds such fun. And I'd have signed the petition – I don't think it's fair someone taking over *our tower*!'

'It's not our tower,' Edie said diplomatically. 'It belonged to Helen's family, and now they've sold it to someone else. So if they've got permission to build a house, then I suppose—'

'Oh, come on, Edie, whose side are you on?' Rose said impatiently.

'I agree – no one's got any right to live in our tower,' Belinda said defiantly. 'I think when they move in we should poison their water supply and let down their tyres!'

Everyone laughed.

'I wonder who it is?' Rose said.

'Probably some stupid rich person,' Sally snorted.

'Why do you think it's someone rich?' Alice said. 'I mean, it's only a little tower.'

But this observation was drowned by a deafening clatter from the streaked sky above, and the girls looked up to see a helicopter circling directly above them.

'Holy Moses!' shrieked Belinda, fumbling for her sketchbook.

'Get back!' Alice shouted, pulling the others towards the hedge. 'It's going to land on top of us!'

'Wave at it!' Edie cried, pulling off her jersey and flapping it wildly in the air.

'Oh, don't be stupid,' Belinda said, craning her neck as she made rapid sketches in her book. 'It's going to land in the field over there.'

'WHERE?'

'OVER THERE!'

Belinda was right, and everyone watched, transfixed, as the helicopter lurched over and came to land in the park, a little beyond the tennis courts.

'That area's an unofficial helipad for Knight's Haddon parents,' Belinda said knowingly as the noise died down. 'When my cousin was here there was a Saudi princess who always came back to school that way.'

'Well, there's no Saudi princess here now,' Alice said. 'Who is it?'

'Anastasia's father?' Belinda suggested. The prince was the only other parent known to have once arrived by helicopter, and that was only after his daughter had been kidnapped.

Edie watched nervously, wondering if the prince had come to inspect the tower – and if Anastasia's secret was about to be blown.

But when the helicopter landed a woman with streaked blonde hair and a tweed cape stepped out, and was helped down the steps by her pilot. Seeing the girls she waved, and beckoned them over.

The girls edged forward warily.

'Hello,' said the woman, pulling close her cape in a protective gesture. 'Are you all escapees from Knight's Haddon?'

'Not escaping exactly,' said Sally, beaming. 'We were just walking back.'

'Of course you are,' said the woman, examining them though narrowed eyes. 'Let me introduce myself. I am

Eustacia – Eustacia Stone – and I wonder if any of you know my daughter Janet?'

'Yes,' said Alice. 'She's in their class,' she explained, pointing at the others, 'and my dorm.'

'Are you looking after her? I do hope so. But where is the beastly child? Why isn't she part of the welcoming posse? Do you think she's in detention?'

'She may not have known you were coming,' Sally said, speaking in an embarrassed rush. 'I mean, it's not an *exeat* weekend, you see, so—'

'She was perfectly aware I was coming,' said Mrs Stone. 'And she knew *exactly* what time to expect me. Everything was arranged.' Her voice was light and dry, but Edie was struck by its lack of warmth. 'People use helicopters precisely because they are time-conscious and need to be punctual. The sky tends to be a little less crowded than the roads,' Mrs Stone added, in case Sally hadn't understood.

Sally blushed. She knew that Janet's mother lived in New York and was the editor of a glossy magazine. These facts, combined with Eustacia Stone's glamorous looks, appeared to excite her extremely.

'Is one of you Anastasia Stolonov?' Eustacia Stone asked, her eyes moving impatiently from one uniformed girl to the next.

'Certainly not!' Sally blurted. 'She's the one who really *is* in detention,' she added – before being silenced by a kick in the shins from Alice. There was a rule at Knight's Haddon that no one was to speak of Anastasia to any outsider.

But Mrs Stone's curiosity seemed to have been aroused. 'Really?' she said. 'Is she naughty then? As naughty as Janet?'

If the question was a trap it was one into which all the girls fell at once, rushing to reassure Mrs Stone that Janet was in a class of her own. All except Alice, who vainly held the line that Janet wasn't bad, just new.

But Eustacia Stone, having set the ball rolling, seemed indifferent to where it landed.

'Are Janet and Anastasia friends?'

All eyes looked to Edie to answer this difficult question. 'I wouldn't say they're particular friends . . .' she said hesitantly.

'What's your name?'

'Edith,' said Edie, with a surprised look.

'Are you the friend of Anastasia who—?'

Edie coloured and Alice stepped in to help her out. 'Edie's friends with both Anastasia and Janet. We all are, really. Everyone's friends with everyone. It's that sort of school.'

'How lovely that sounds, if a touch unlikely,' said Mrs Stone, with a smile that failed to reach her eyes. 'Now, girls, perhaps one of you could ring Janet? Meanwhile, who's for tea? Bubbly and smoked salmon sandwiches? Gaston!' she said with a wave of her hand. 'Could you produce the goodies and find somewhere vaguely flat to lay out the rug?'

Gaston was the pilot. He looked almost like a child, Edie thought, and very cold in his blue blazer and white trousers. Edie wondered if it was Eustacia Stone who insisted he wear such stupid clothes.

'I *love* smoked salmon sandwiches!' said Sally.

'But – but we'll be late,' said Alice, looking at her watch. 'And we can't drink bubbly,' she added quickly.

'And we don't have phones,' said Edie, as Gaston produced the hamper.

'Darlings, do you mean you are all obedient to that mad rule about mobiles? How completely quaint! As for the drink, I'm twelve years sober, you sillies. It's sparkling elderflower. Oh—' Her voice changed suddenly, making her sound less in charge. 'Look who's coming to join us.'

The others followed the direction of her glance and saw Janet trailing across the field with Miss Fotheringay at her side.

Edie was struck by the cold look with which Janet greeted her mother, and by Eustacia Stone's glassy smile as she shook Miss Fotheringay's hand. She did not kiss her daughter.

'Good morning, Mrs Stone,' Miss Fotheringay said. 'I see you have gathered several of our pupils about you while the one you came to see was looking for you on the other side of the school.'

'She has no sense of direction,' Mrs Stone said, looking with evident curiosity at Miss Fotheringay's old tweed coat and mud-caked boots. 'I'm hoping you might give her one. We send them here to be polished, after all.'

Everyone looked embarrassed by the abruptness of her manner – everyone except Janet, who glanced at

Edie with raised eyes. *Didn't I tell you my mother was a monster?* her expression seemed to say.

'We do our best,' Miss Fotheringay replied, in an even voice. 'Now, I'm sure you're in a hurry to get away.'

Eustacia hesitated a moment, glancing at the hamper – but then she seemed to think better of the picnic she had planned. 'I certainly am,' she replied, gesturing Gaston to retrieve the hamper from the grass. 'Helicopters and hurry go together like a horse and carriage. Good-bye, girls!' she said, blowing kisses as she clambered inside. 'So interesting to meet you all. Come on, Janet darling, let's fly!'

Think What You Like!

Inside the school girls crowded around the windows, watching as the helicopter lifted off from the park.

'Anastasia! Look at this!' said Phoebe, who was crouched alone on the dormitory windowsill when Anastasia rushed in. 'It's unbelievable! Janet's mother—'

'Where is she?' Anastasia demanded.

'Who?'

'*Edie!*' Anastasia said in a choking voice, looking wildly around at the empty beds.

Phoebe shrugged. 'I don't know.' Then, 'Anastasia! Wait! What's up?'

But Anastasia had fled.

Anastasia ran and ran, through the North Tower, the East Tower, the South and the West, hardly aware of the faces that gazed after her in bewilderment as she raced past.

'Edie!' she cried, flinging open the door to the lower school common room, where a group of first years looked up, startled, from their game of cards. 'Edie!' she sobbed, tearing into the dining room, where only Miss Mannering and the head cook remained, sitting at the high table, their heads bent over a spreadsheet of the week's menu.

'Anastasia! What on earth do you think you are doing?' Miss Mannering demanded, looking up with protruding eyes. But Anastasia had gone, vanished like a wisp, leaving only the frantic clatter of her footsteps echoing through the stone arch.

'Hey, don't run!' shouted a prefect, as Anastasia pelted through a group of indignant sixth-formers in the hall. 'Anastasia Stolonov, come back here!'

But the child fled on in a fury, to the science laboratory, to her empty classroom, then to the cloakroom, swishing her arm through the line of hanging duffel coats as if expecting to find Edie crouched behind one. 'Edie!' she shouted, as she ran on blindly to the music wing, and flung open the doors on to the empty practice rooms. 'Edie! Edie! *Edie!*' she cried, in a voice choked with tears.

A bell clattered through her distress, and Anastasia looked down from the landing window to see a stream of girls dressed in navy blue tracksuits pour out of a coach stationed in the drive.

The lacrosse team, she thought dully, watching as they trooped inside; then she gave a gasp as another figure appeared in the courtyard below.

'Edie!' she cried, flying like a whirlwind down the narrow, spiral stairs. As she spun off the bottom step into the corridor she was aware of a serene figure in a swirling skirt floating towards her, smiling beneath a mass of flowing red hair. *Mrs Prentice*, she thought dimly as she hurtled straight into her.

'Anastasia!' yelped Mrs Prentice, gasping with fright as her tin of paint fell and splattered across the stone floor. But Anastasia ran on without stopping, so fast that the art mistress did not hear her garbled apology, and did not see the demon in her eyes.

Edie hurried across the courtyard in the fading light. Her happy afternoon had left her determined to make up with Anastasia. Their friendship was too deep to start rowing about nothing.

Anastasia had been difficult all term but there was a reason for that. Edie knew how her friend's mind worked –Anastasia was trying so hard not to brood about the big things that she couldn't control, such as the prospect of her mother coming to live at the tower, that she was giving all her attention to little things which didn't matter.

Such as whether or not Edie really cared tuppence for the stupid ferrets! The important thing, surely, was that she'd been making sure they were looked after properly. She didn't have to *like* them too.

I should help her though, not fight with her, she thought as she made her way to the animal house. She was sure

Anastasia would have gone there after their row in the common room. Even though it was out of bounds for her, she would have found a way to sneak out.

But Edie had just started through the rose garden when she turned to see Anastasia pounding up the pathway behind her, her face lit by a livid flush.

'Did you do it?' she sobbed. 'Did you? Just tell me, Edie, tell me, please!'

Edie looked at her in bewilderment. 'What, Anastasia? What are you talking about?'

'Did you?' Anastasia demanded, her voice rising. '*Was it you?*'

Edie shook her head, not knowing what she was denying. She glanced down the path, wondering if Rose and Belinda might burst from the bushes and tell her that it was all some game. But then her eyes returned, helpless, to Anastasia's contorted face.

Something in her friend's expression made Edie's heart dull, and when she spoke her own voice sounded studiedly calm. 'Ansti, please, can't you see I don't know what you're talking about. Whatever's wrong I'll help you, you know I will, but you must tell me what's happened.'

'Where were you?' Anastasia raged.

'Where was I when?' Edie asked quietly.

'At lunch. All this afternoon. Ever since Janet went off in that stupid helicopter. Where were you?'

'In the library,' Edie answered truthfully. 'I had to finish that boring Latin prep. Why?' she said then.

'You know why! And you're lying!'

'Please, Anastasia. Whatever you're upset about, tell me, instead of shouting like a drama queen.'

Edie regretted it as soon as she'd said it. 'Drama Queen' was what everyone had called Anastasia last year, when a teacher had been secretly persecuting her.

Anastasia began to shake. 'How could you, Edie! How *could* you!'

'How could I *what*?' Edie asked calmly.

'You did it! You let them out! It was you, it must have been you. *Look!*' Anastasia turned and pointed with a savage jab at the animal house that stood at the top of the path, its door swinging open in the breeze. 'My ferrets have gone! I went there just after lunch and they'd gone! Someone let them out! I suppose you think it's funny, but it's not, Edie, it's sick!'

Edie stared at the animal house stupidly, and then at Anastasia, her eyes moving back and forth from the swinging door to her friend's trembling face. 'I didn't, Ansti, I didn't do it,' was all she said.

'Just because you didn't like them you let them go! Just because . . . just because you thought they looked like Lyle!' Anastasia lunged forward and fell on Edie with pounding fists. 'We were best friends, Edie, best friends!' she sobbed, pummelling at her with pitiful blows. 'We were best friends, but you never cared, never! You couldn't have done or you wouldn't have let them go.'

Edie raised her hands, trying to fend off the blows, then finally seized Anastasia by the wrists.

'Get off!' Anastasia shouted, pulling free. 'They

warned me! They all warned me and I should have listened, because it's true. It's true, Edie, and I should have seen it. The only person you care about is Miss Fotheringay! I know you told her about the horse fair! It's because of you that I'm being humiliated like this – gated all term while you lot get to have fun! And now this! What's wrong with you, Edie! Why do you hate me so much? What have I *done*?'

Edie watched, speechless, as Anastasia stormed off down the path. Then she heard voices and turned, startled, to see Mrs Prentice approaching with a group of first formers who were lugging painting easels and canvas bags.

Edie couldn't face talking to anyone. On an instinct she turned and raced up the slope towards the animal house, and slipped inside. When she turned on the light she saw the door of the ferrets' cage swinging open, their china feeding dish lying broken on the floor.

She wondered with a wild hope if it was a spiteful joke, and someone had simply sneaked in and moved Anastasia's ferrets to another cage. *The sort of joke Phoebe would play*, Edie thought, as she lay on the floor and craned her head beneath the bottom shelf of cages, her eyes searching through the filth of cobwebs and straw.

'Treasure! Precious!' she called, softly at first, as if by cajoling them with Anastasia's silly names they might come wriggling out in surrender, but then finally she sat back up on her heels in despair. 'Precious! Treasure! Where are you, you revolting, trouble-making Things –

where are you, you creeps!' She saw a lop-eared rabbit blinking at her sedately from its hut, and glared at it in fury. 'Oh, go *away*!' she shouted, thrusting her face up to the wire meshing.

'Edie, my dear child, whatever is going on?'

Edie swung round, to see Mrs Prentice in the door-way. 'Nothing, Mrs Prentice,' she mumbled, scrambling to her feet.

'Well, hurry up, dear – you'll be late for supper.'

The teacher waited until Edie had come out, then took only a brief glance inside the animal house before closing the door for the night. She did not seem to notice anything wrong, and Edie was too shaken to tell her that the ferrets had gone.

She would find out soon enough though – and so would everyone else, Edie reflected grimly.

But who could have let them go?

Edie decided to give supper a miss. Instead she returned to the library, and hid herself at a corner desk. It was less the loss of the ferrets than Anastasia's accusations that had shocked her. She sat with her reading lamp unlit, aware of an unnatural quickness in her breath, as if her body had been violently shaken. She was not conscious of the time passing, but sat staring at nothing until a bell summoned her to bed.

Rose and Belinda were outside the bathroom cubicles, clutching their towels and sponge bags as they stood huddled in conversation with two third years, but when they saw Edie they all melted away.

Edie felt sick. She knew from their sly looks that

Anastasia must have told them she had done it – that she'd turned Anastasia's ferrets loose.

She walked on, past the laundry room, and heard voices from inside, arguing about the bath rota:

'Belinda was s'posed to be in cubicle four at five past seven, but she didn't get out until quarter to eight so I missed my bath. I don't know what she was doing in there . . . she must have been soaking for hours!'

'She probably fell asleep, you know what she's like.'

'She can't have, unless she's turned into a whale. I had a bath half an hour ago and the water was freezing!'

'She is a whale!' the other snorted.

'Hey,' said the first one. 'I meant to tell you something. Did you hear Matron earlier talking to Miss Pickering? Last weekend someone raided the kitchen and lots of food went missing – eggs and sausages. Do you think someone's had a secret barbecue?'

'Well, if they did, *I* wasn't invited,' said the other in a huff. 'Who do you think might know . . . ?'

Edie felt a momentary relief – they weren't all talking about her, after all! But when the girls emerged from the laundry room holding their weekly issue of towels, they looked embarrassed to see her and hurried away.

When she returned to her own dormitory Sally and Alice greeted her with questioning looks.

So Anastasia's told everyone it was me! Edie thought bitterly. What did they expect her to do? Fall to her knees, and plead her innocence in a trembling voice? Was there a set script for people accused of releasing two ferrets belonging to a spoilt Russian princess? But

Edie was in no mood for speeches.

'Well? What are you two staring at?' she said furiously as she tossed herself on her bed.

Sally and Alice were silent.

'God, what's wrong with everyone?' Edie took her book from her bedside table and slammed it open on her pillow. 'If you think I did it, why not say so? Or call the RSPCA – or the police? Go on, why don't you?'

'Edie,' Alice said gently, 'we haven't said anything.'

'You didn't say it, but you obviously think it was me or you wouldn't look at me like that!'

Alice looked embarrassed – but Sally seemed to be relishing the drama.

'Apparently it happened at night,' she said, watching Edie slyly.

Edie's eyes spun at her: 'How do you know?'

'Process of elimination,' Sally said coolly. 'The ferrets were definitely there yesterday evening – Anastasia sneaked out after supper to feed them. And Mr Wilcox told the Prent that when he went up to the animal house this morning the door was wide open!'

Edie brooded. Mr Wilcox was the groundsman. If he found the shed door swinging open in the morning, that certainly pointed to the ferrets having been released by night.

'But *who*?' she began, puzzling out loud – then stopped as she saw Sally throw Alice a meaningful look. She felt a rush of blood to her head. 'Go on, say it!' she shouted, marching over to Sally's bed. 'Say it! Come out with it, instead of just giving me dirty looks!'

'Edie, we're not accusing you,' said Alice gently. 'We just wonder—'

'Of course you're accusing me. Your looks, your silence—'

'Keep your hair on, Edie,' Sally said unkindly, hearing the break in Edie's voice.

But Edie's hair was gone. 'You're pathetic!' she shouted, red in the face. 'Anastasia could tell you I'd eaten her revolting ferrets for breakfast and you'd believe her! Well, go on then, think it! Think what you like! I don't care!'

Edie was still in the bathroom when Matron arrived in the dormitory corridor ten minutes later for one of her routine tidiness checks.

'What is that?' she said, pointing to a yellow games sock on the floor.

'Sorry,' Alice mumbled, picking it up.

'Where's Miss Edith Wilson?' Matron said, pointing to a mess of clothes on Edie's bed.

'Bath number five,' Sally replied.

Matron looked tersely at her watch. 'Perhaps then you could go and enquire how long she intends to stay there – and kindly remind her that this is an English boarding school, not a Turkish bath. Now, can anyone tell me to whom this dressing gown belongs to? It appears to have gone on a cross-country walk and ended up in the bathroom at the end of the corridor.' As she spoke Matron held aloft Edie's scarlet fleece, the hem of which was caked in mud.

Alice and Sally exchanged glances.

Then, 'It's Edie's,' Alice said.

'Well, you can tell her I've taken it to be washed,' Matron said, and bustled away.

Zip Lip

When Edie walked into breakfast next morning she knew that her guilt was an established fact.

The other second years were already huddled around their familiar table in the far corner, and when they saw her their conversation stopped. She could feel people looking at her – but no one caught her eye.

Edie turned, blushing, to the serving hatch and helped herself as slowly as she could to toast and coffee, sensing the silence in the room. She took her breakfast to an empty table, where no one joined her.

As she ate, she reflected on how stupidly she had behaved. When Anastasia had accused her of letting the ferrets go she should have followed her back to school at once, and insisted to everyone that she hadn't done it.

Instead she had hidden in the library, like a guilty child.

And as for her outburst in the dormitory. '*Think what you like!*' They would have taken that to mean guilty as charged, Edie thought bitterly. But a stubbornness had taken hold of her. If they thought she had released the ferrets, then let them accuse her of it to her face.

Until then, why should she defend herself for something she hadn't done?

But no one did accuse her. In fact, no one spoke to her at all, and Edie spent the day skulking on her own in the dormitory – where Janet found her lying on her bed before supper.

'You've flown back,' Edie commented dully.

'No. My mother put me on a train at Paddington. And what's up with you?' Janet asked, shaking sweets on to her bed.

Edie looked up, uncertain. She knew how much Janet had cared about the ferrets, so she supposed she would hate her too.

'Phoebe's told me everything,' Janet added, sitting on her bed. 'Don't worry, Edie. The Things will be fine. They belong in the wild.'

'But you loved them!'

'All the more reason—' said Janet, then stopped. 'Why does everyone think you did it?' she asked then. 'That's what I don't understand.'

Edie explained, brokenly, about the row with Anastasia on Saturday morning.

'I said I wanted to set them free, but of course I didn't mean that. I wouldn't even know if they'd be all right in the wild or not, and I would never do that to her, however cross I was. But then when she found they'd gone, she assumed it was me!'

'Didn't you tell her that it wasn't?'

'Yes,' Edie said simply. 'But she didn't believe me.'

'I see,' Janet said slowly. 'And now she's got the whole year on her side?'

Edie nodded. 'The whole school, more like. Even the sixth-formers give me odd looks.'

'Well, I believe you,' Janet said.

Edie looked at her sharply. 'Really?'

'Of course. Anyone who thinks you did it is an idiot. Betray your beloved Princess Anastasia? You wouldn't dare!'

Edie managed a feeble smile. She could take any amount of teasing, so long as someone was on her side. 'When I find out who did do it,' she said, 'I'll—' Her face hardened.

'What?'

'I don't know. But whoever they are I hate them more than I've ever hated anyone. Imagine doing that, then letting someone else take the rap.'

'So who do you think it was?'

'I've no idea, but someone who has it in for Anastasia, I suppose.'

Janet shrugged. 'Then you'd better put me on your suspect list. I've got it in for her! I think it's unforgivable, going around blaming you to everyone, when she hasn't a shred of proof!'

'She's upset,' Edie said, surprised to find herself

defending her. 'She'll believe me when she calms down.'

'Maybe,' Janet said. 'But really, Wilson, you shouldn't stand for it. You're a far better friend to her than she deserves.'

Edie could not help sometimes agreeing with Janet during the wretched week that followed. She felt that everyone was avoiding her, and in the dormitory even Alice spoke to her coldly and suspiciously. Edie was shaken at how easily people accepted her guilt, without any evidence other than Anastasia's word.

She was so lonely she almost looked forward to being hauled to the headmistress's office for an interrogation: surely Fothy at least would accuse Edie to her face. But no summons came. It was as though Fothy too was determined to ignore her.

It was something to have Janet on her side, though Newgirl's behaviour continued to baffle.

On Saturday Edie was reading on her bed in the dormitory when Janet came in and changed into her home clothes.

'What are you doing?' Edie asked. The morning's lessons had just finished, but the girls were not allowed to change out of their uniform until after lunch.

'I'm going out,' said Janet. 'I'll see you later.'

'Out?' Edie protested. 'But you know we're not allowed out until two o'clock.'

'Knowing is one thing,' said Janet. 'Caring, quite another.'

'But you're mad. You'll definitely be caught,' Edie said,

sitting up. 'And then you'll be gated and that will be really boring – for me,' she ended sheepishly.

'I like it when you tell the truth, Wilson,' said Janet, with an affectionate ruffle of Edie's hair. 'But I'm afraid it doesn't quite swing it for me, all the same.'

Edie was puzzled. Even by Janet's standards, sneaking out to the village before lunch, and without a walking partner, seemed an oddly reckless thing to do. She wondered why she was so intent on going on her own, instead of waiting for the others – Edie was sure Janet's absence would be noticed at lunch.

But Janet was in luck, for the eagle-eyed Miss Mannering did not appear in the dining room that day, and Mr Robinson, who took her place at the end of the long table, seemed too flustered with the responsibility of serving the lamb pie to notice Janet's empty seat.

After lunch Edie returned to the dormitory. She felt annoyed with Janet for having gone off without her. Edie would have liked to walk to the village, but she was certainly not going to ask any of her silent accusers if she could go with them, and she was too proud to tag along with some first years. She would just have to settle for *Tess of the d'Urbervilles* she thought, with a touch of self-pity which melted away as the story drew her in. For a happy couple of hours she forgot about school and instead imagined being Tess in a white dress covered in splashes of horse blood. She wanted to cry out when she went off with Alec d'Urberville. He was so obviously a villain! Suddenly, looking up, she saw Newgirl framed in the doorway.

'Search party?'

'Not that I know of,' Edie replied, shaking herself back into the present.

'Told you I'd get away with it,' said Janet, tossing a pair of gloves on to the bed.

'I wish you'd waited – I had no one to go with,' Edie replied, putting down her book. 'Anyway, what did you buy? Anything for me?'

'Buy?' Janet looked puzzled. 'Where would I . . . ? Oh, tuck, you mean. Sorry, I didn't think of it.'

Edie looked at her suspiciously. 'Where have you been, Janet?'

'Village,' said Janet quickly. 'Where else?'

Edie knew she was lying. 'Why don't you tell me where you really went?'

Janet was silent for a moment. 'Just because—' she began, then stopped. Then – 'Tell me this, Wilson,' she said, nodding at the book lying open on Edie's bed. 'How far have you got with *Tess of the d'Urbervilles*? Or do you know the story anyway?'

'I've only just started it,' said Edie, confused by the change of tack. 'How would I know the story anyway?'

'Most people know the film.'

'Oh,' said Edie dully. She had never seen the films 'most people' knew. 'I still don't see what *Tess of the d'Urbervilles* has got to do with you not telling me stuff.'

'*Tess* is a story about the truth ruining everything. If you want people to like you, there are some things you've got to hold back.'

Edie looked at Janet thoughtfully, remembering how secretive she herself had been when she had first arrived at Knight's Haddon – and how lonely her secrecy had made her. Everything had got better when she had learnt how to be open – until this term, anyway.

'Is that really what you think?' she said quietly.

Janet looked away. 'I'm afraid to tell you stuff, Wilson, and that's not because I don't like you – it's because I do. I like you the best of anyone here. There just happen to be some things I can't tell you.'

'I suppose you think I'll sneak to Fothy!' Edie said crossly.

'Oh, don't be stupid,' Janet replied. 'I wouldn't be your friend if I thought you were like that. But it's true I don't want to get you into trouble.'

Edie was intrigued. But she judged it best not to press for more information now. 'Whatever. You don't have to tell me what you were doing. It's not my business. And it's not as if I haven't got enough else to worry about.'

'Like what?'

'Anastasia's ferrets, of course,' Edie said grimly. 'If I could only find out who did it.'

Janet looked impatient. 'Anastasia's the false friend in this story. Why has she turned on you?'

Because she's jealous, Edie thought, but did not say. She couldn't bear to expose Anastasia to Newgirl's scorn on that front.

'OK,' said Janet, shrugging. 'We won't talk about your darling Anastasia who doesn't want anything to do with you. But tell me this, what are you doing for the *exeat* next weekend?'

Edie had been trying not to think about the *exeat*. Normally she would have spent the weekend with Anastasia and her father in London, or with Miss Fotheringay – but now Anastasia was to be spending the weekend with Fothy, so both Edie's escape routes were gone.

'I suppose I'll be going to my cousins in Devon,' she said glumly.

'Great,' said Janet. 'Can I come with you?'

'Come with me? Are you mad?'

'My mother's back in New York and told me to fix something with a friend. But if you don't want me . . .' Janet's voice trailed off.

'It's not that,' Edie reassured her. 'I just can't imagine anyone wanting to come to Folly Farm. It's pretty . . . horrible.'

Janet smiled. 'Horror shared is horror halved. And if I don't make a plan then that bonkers headmistress might suggest I spend the weekend with her.' Janet shuddered.

And then I'll come back from Folly and find you and Anastasia best friends, Edie thought grimly. But still she hesitated. She had never taken anyone from Knight's Haddon to Folly Farm. It was such a hated place to her that she hardly even talked about it at school, as if by not talking about it she could pretend it wasn't real.

But it was no use pretending now. Short of a miracle, Edie would be on the train back to Devon in a week's time. She had a sudden vision of Lyle, his ferret-like face weaving through the crowd on the station platform, peering into her carriage. And then she thought that it mightn't be so bad if she had Janet with her. Janet wouldn't be frightened of Lyle. They could see him off together.

'Do come. I'd like that,' she said, with a feeling of quiet daring.

For the next few days, Janet and Edie did everything together. It occurred to Edie that, although *she* had been delegated to look out for *Janet*, it was much more a case of Janet who was looking out for her – if only to lure her into trouble.

Somehow, whenever there was a lesson to get to, or a hockey practice to attend, or a bell summoning everyone to lunch or tea or supper or bed, Edie would find Janet sweeping her off in the wrong direction.

'Hey, where are we going?' Edie asked on Monday afternoon, when she found herself being spirited into a music room while the rest of the school trooped dutifully into lunch.

'Against the flow,' Janet replied, smirking, as she pulled Edie inside and locked the door.

Something told Edie that the flow wasn't worth fighting – especially if it meant missing lunch. But the row with Anastasia had wrung something from her, and she found herself following Janet without protest. After a few days, being in trouble seemed perfectly routine. Even when Miss Mannering put her and Janet in detention for missing assembly, Edie didn't care.

Order marks and detentions seemed trivial things when she knew that the whole year was talking about her, saying horrid things behind her back.

On Thursday afternoon she was fishing for a packet of chewing gum in her pocket when she became aware of footsteps quickening on her from behind.

'Edith. May I have a word?'

Edie's heart sank. A command phrased as a question. That was Fothy's way.

'You have been testing my debating skills, Edith,' Miss Fotheringay said, once her study door was closed.

'Your debating skills?' Edie asked nervously.

Miss Fotheringay nodded. 'I used to debate in the Cambridge Union. "This House Believes that under tyranny it is right to rebel." We won,' the headmistress recalled, smiling.

Edie wondered which side of the debate she had been on.

'And now,' Miss Fotheringay continued, flourishing a letter, "This House Believes that Edith Wilson and Janet Stone should be sent home until the end of term."'

Edie sucked in her breath. For all the trouble she had been in, this possibility had not struck her.

Miss Fotheringay sighed, as if bored of the argument already. 'I can assure you, Edith, I am fighting your pitch as hard as I can. But if you insist on skipping assembly, and twittering with Janet through every class, then I am afraid my rhetorical skills might not be up to defending you.'

Edie turned crimson, hearing how foolish it sounded – and the thought of being sent back to Folly Farm until the end of term made her stomach turn. The *exeat* would be bad enough.

'Of course I shall continue to do everything I can to keep your executioners at bay,' Miss Fotheringay went on, her voice like steel.

Edie looked at Miss Fotheringay uncertainly, hearing the taunts of the other girls ringing in her ears:

Edie can do no wrong . . .

She could come down to breakfast in her pyjamas and Fothy would just smile.

'Not least,' Miss Fotheringay went on, 'because I partly blame myself for the trouble you're in. It was wrong of me putting you in charge of a new girl, as if Anastasia's demands on you weren't enough.'

'But – I was glad,' Edie said truthfully.

'You could not have seen what a burden it would be,' Miss Fotheringay corrected her. 'Janet has been determined to disgrace herself and she has led you astray. Tell me, Edith, why is she so bent on getting into trouble?'

Edie remembered Janet's words on the first day of term: *'I'm going to get myself chucked out . . . shouldn't be difficult if it's as strict as all that . . .'*

'I don't know,' Edie said, her thoughts leading back to Saturday, when Janet had disappeared for nearly three hours. She was glad now that Janet hadn't told her what she had been up to – otherwise Fothy would have tried to wheedle it out of her. She looked at the headmistress with studied blankness, determined not to be used as a spy.

Miss Fotheringay drew herself up and walked to the door. 'All right Zip Lip,' she said. 'You'd better return to prep.'

A Rude Awakening

The next morning the whole school was woken by a piercing shriek.

'Fire alarm practice,' Sally groaned, tossing off her duvet. 'Why do they have to do it in the middle of the night? As if we didn't have to get up early enough as it was.'

Edie looked at her watch. It was not yet five. When she pulled back the curtains she could see torchlights in the pitch-dark courtyard below, dancing to the shrill of the siren, and when she looked across the park she could just make out the tip of the Prefects' Tower, pale white in the moonlight.

She remembered her first term at Knight's Haddon, when she had seen the tower on fire.

'What if it's real?' she said, fumbling for her slippers.

'It's not real, it's only a drill,' said Alice, who in her sleepiness seemed to forget that Edie was in Coventry. 'Don't you remember – Matron let slip we'd be having one sometime this week? Trust Fothy to choose the coldest night of term. Now hurry up, everyone,' she went on, taking charge. A second alarm had started and they could hear footsteps hurrying along the corridor outside.

'You're to take yourselves to your assembly points with all possible speed,' came Matron's voice. 'But *don't* you be thinking of running now!'

'Where is our assembly point?' asked Janet, who was the last to heave herself out of bed.

'By the netball courts, I'll show you,' Alice said in her form captain's tone. 'And where's your dressing gown? It's going to be like the Arctic out there.'

'Fire drill is basically a dressing-gown beauty contest,' explained Sally, warming to the occasion. 'Fothy always wears a different one – she must have a whole wardrobe full of them! But look out for the Man. Hers is a revolting orangey-pink affair in quilted nylon!' She flashed herself a quick look in the mirror, as if to make sure she would pass muster in her anticipated parade. 'Some of the sixth-formers have silk ones!' she said wistfully, as she hurried after Alice to the door.

'Well, I pity anyone in a silk dressing gown on a night like this,' Alice said sensibly.

'Please, come on – last time Matron put two dormitories on early bedtime for the rest of term for being late.'

'Dressing gown, dressing down, I haven't got one,'

Janet said languidly.

'Use mine,' Edie said, chucking her the scarlet fleece.

'What will you wear?'

'Jersey and long johns,' Edie replied. 'That thing's too long for me anyway. It'll trip me up in the dark.'

The girls from the other dormitories were already stampeding down the corridor when Edie's dormitory emerged. There were fire escapes on all sides of the school. The one in the South Tower – their tower – was overhung with creepers, and took a wriggly route down the side of the building, eventually landing in the kitchen garden where some of the senior girls had their own small plots of ground – coveted miniature allotments where they were encouraged to grow all manner of exotic things. The gardeners of the fourth and fifth stood guard with their torches, shouting crossly as the second years tramped over their carefully-hoed beds on the way to the assembly point.

'Hey, don't step there – it's the beginning of my salad crop!'

'Look out, you clod! You're treading on my artichokes!'

Edie had a torch, but several of the other second years had forgotten theirs in the rush to get outside, and she found a group of girls gathered behind her as she lit the way along the thin, frosted paths.

'Oh, I hate fire drill!' wailed Belinda, skirting round the compost heap. 'Why do we always have to do it in the dark?'

'It's spooky,' agreed Rose, giving a theatrical shudder.

'My mother says Knight's Haddon's haunted,' Sally

said knowingly. 'When she was here one of the sixth-formers saw a ghost in the laundry room!'

Edie listened in scorn. She didn't believe in ghosts. But when she looked back at the school now, she was struck by something eerie in its appearance, with its dark towers, and its pointed windows glinting through black creeper.

'Edie, get a move on!' someone said from behind.

Edie tramped on, lighting the way with her torch. But she found her thoughts turning again to the ferrets, as if the moonlight were teasing her with the mystery she had failed to solve.

Who could have done it? Another girl? A mistress? Or did Knight's Haddon have secret phantoms of its own? She kept glancing back towards the school, as if the silent building might whisper a clue, then she saw a light come on in the window at the top of the West Tower. Edie looked up at it furtively: it was Miss Fotheringay's bedroom, and as she watched she saw the curtains draw apart, and the tall, stone-like figure of the headmistress appear silhouetted against the glass.

'Oi!' Edie gasped, as someone bashed into her from behind, knocking the torch from her hands. She picked it up and went on, out of the kitchen garden and on to the wide lawn that sloped into the park.

'Hey, Edie, hurry up! The second-year counting point is over there!'

Edie shook her head and tripped on after the others.

'I'm going to tell Papa that they make us get out of bed in the middle of the night and go outside with no clothes on, in February!' she heard Anastasia fume. 'He's always worrying about me getting a cold – he'll have something to say to Fothy about that!' Then, 'Achooo!' she added indignantly.

'Fothy will be sorry when we all die of pneumonia!' Belinda sympathized. 'Anyway, where is she?'

'Probably tucked up in bed,' speculated Phoebe. 'Sipping cocoa while the rest of us freeze!'

Everyone agreed that five o'clock on a winter's morning seemed cruel timing for a fire drill – but Edie noticed that one girl at least seemed to be enjoying it, and that was Janet, who was dancing about the lawn in Edie's dressing gown, patting her mouth while making Hiawatha-like chants to the din of the siren.

While the others stumbled and shivered, Janet seemed suddenly to have burst to life like a wild animal.

'Janet! Stop clowning around or you'll get us all in detention!' Alice called out, urging the others to the assembly point. Edie watched in grudging admiration as Janet tossed down her torch and turned a lop-sided cartwheel in the grass, before sashaying back into line.

Miss Mannering was waiting with her clipboard when the girls reached the netball court, and seemed oblivious to the titters aroused by her lurid pink gown.

'Six minutes,' she announced, consulting a stopwatch as she scored off the last name on her list. 'That is a disgrace. As first years you managed to evacuate the North Wing in less than four. Tonight you have reduced your evacuation speed by more than two minutes. And had this had been a real fire,' Miss Mannering continued dramatically, 'two minutes could have made the difference between life and death. Sally!' she demanded, pointing a torch in her face. 'Of what material is the interior of Knight's Haddon primarily constructed?'

'Wood,' Sally replied dronishly – the girls all knew Miss Mannering's fire-drill lecture by heart.

'Wood. Indeed,' Miss Mannering said impatiently. 'And wood is . . .'

'Highly flammable,' Edie found herself reciting in a sing-song tone.

'Correct,' Miss Mannering said, switching the torch to shine at Edie. 'Though I will thank you not to address me in that sarcastic voice. I can assure you that if a real fire were to break out at Knight's Haddon the flammable condition of the building would become a matter of the utmost pertinence. If a fire had broken out in the kitchens, those of you billeted in the South Tower dormitories would have been especially vulnerable. Dawdlers,' Miss Mannering concluded evocatively, 'would have been engulfed by flames. Do I make myself clear?'

'Yes, Miss Mannering,' everyone chorused as a collective shiver ran through the ranks.

But then Miss Mannering's eye was caught by something across the netball court, and she spun round. The others followed her gaze to see Janet skipping away from them, her head tossed back and her arms flung out in abandon. As everyone watched her in astonishment, she twirled her torch to the skies and let out a shrill whoop of joy, like a wolf braying to the moonlight.

'Janet Stone! Come here this instant!' Miss Mannering shouted. 'What on earth do you think you are playing at? This is a fire drill, not a dancing class!'

'Sorr-eee!' Janet replied cheerfully, returning across the court at a leisurely skip.

Everyone giggled nervously, astonished at Janet's daring. As she approached, her torch flickered across the teacher's face, which Edie noted had turned an ominous shade.

'Janet Stone, stand over there!' Miss Mannering said fiercely, pointing to the goalpost. 'Alice, you will kindly take the register to Mrs Prentice.'

Janet did not look at all chastened by Miss Mannering's telling-off. She slouched against the goalpost as if in a world of her own, twirling her torch at the stars. Edie watched her curiously, envying her indifference.

'Oh, by geez – look at Mr Robinson!' Phoebe whistled, as the maths teacher appeared in a flowing white gown.

Everyone tittered. 'I wish I had my sketchbook!' Belinda said, her eyes drinking him in.

'Whooooo! He looks just like a pantomime ghost!' someone else called.

Edie listened to the laughter and looked wistfully at Anastasia, wondering if she was sharing in the joke – but Anastasia was standing very still, staring at Janet as if transfixed.

Janet Changes Tack

When the fire drill was over the girls tumbled back into their beds.

Edie went straight to sleep, and dreamt that she and Janet were ferrets, frolicking together in a cage. Edie had just nipped Janet's tail when she looked up and saw Anastasia staring at them accusingly through the mesh.

'I'm not Precious – I'm Edie!' Edie shouted – then woke up to see Janet laughing down at her.

'You're Edie, *and* you're precious!' Janet said, flicking her with water from a tooth mug. 'Now, hurry up or we'll miss breakfast. And it may be the last meal of the day,' she replied. 'Though I assume you've been exaggerating about the conditions at Folly Farm.'

Edie gathered her wits with a groan. The day of the *exeat* had dawned already.

The dining room was beginning to empty when Edie and Janet arrived. The promise of a weekend's freedom had brought a mood of high spirits, as girls clattered their empty breakfast plates on to the hatch, and rushed back to their dormitories to collect their bags.

'Anastasia was here looking for you,' said Alice, hurrying past as Edie was sitting with deliberate slowness over her porridge.

'We told her that you were getting the station bus, and that Janet was going with you to Devon – and she suddenly shot off again,' Sally explained, deigning to talk to her.

'Where—' Edie began, but Sally had charged away. Edie wondered why Anastasia had been looking for her. They hadn't spoken for nearly two weeks.

But the mention of Anastasia's name seemed to make Janet even more impatient to be gone. 'Come on, slow-coach,' she said, looking at her watch. 'The bus goes at nine.'

'You're the one who's always late,' Edie said sullenly.

'Not when it's a getaway bus,' Janet smiled.

Four hours later Edie stood alone on the platform of the small country station, her eyes scouring the dwindling crowd.

'She's always late,' she said gloomily, when Janet reappeared from the station shop.

'Well, there's no point hanging around here,' Janet said, stashing chocolate bars into her rucksack. 'Come on, let's start walking. I've got some supplies.'

'Walking?'

'Why not? You said the house wasn't far from the station,' Janet said, as she swung her bag on to her shoulder. 'Or would you sooner stand here freezing to death?'

Edie hesitated, remembering her terrified flight along the road when she had run away from her cousins, and the sound of Lyle's wolfish laugh as he had crept up on her from behind.

But just as they were walking through the ticket hall, a harassed-looking Aunt Sophia swung towards them through the glass doors, her red hair tumbling unkempt from beneath the hood of a wax coat.

'Ah, there you are!' she said, as though Edie and Janet were the ones who were late. 'I've had such a business getting here with that ruddy horsebox. I could kill Tony for not arranging things better!' Aunt Sophia bent her cheek to Edie for a kiss, while she looked at Janet with an expression of cursory curiosity. 'You must be Juliet, so sweet of you to come and see us. I do hope you won't be bored. What I mean is, I'm afraid you will be awfully bored, but I hope you won't hold it against us. Edie hates it at Folly, don't you, darling?' she went on, talking over her shoulder as she led them to the car. 'But at least you can entertain each other. Perhaps you'd like to go out riding? That would be a turn-up for the books. I've just collected a new mare who desperately needs to be taken out, and Lyle—'

'You know I don't ride,' said Edie, traipsing behind with her suitcase. 'And her name is Janet.'

'No, it's not,' said Aunt Sophia, 'it's Jeanie. Stupid name for a horse, I agree, but the man who sold her to me said it was bad luck to change it.'

'I wasn't talking about the horse,' Edie replied.

'But let's,' said Janet, running towards the horsebox and peering inside. 'Oh, she's lovely! Wow, she must be fifteen hands at least! I'd love to ride her.'

'Are you experienced?' Aunt Sophia asked, interested, as she motioned the girls into the cab of the horsebox. 'This one's a bit of a kicker.'

'Oh, I don't mind,' Janet said eagerly. 'I'm used to them like that.'

'Well, you'd better go out on the pony first, he's easier to handle. But I'm sure Tony will give you a go on Jeanie.' Aunt Sophia glanced at Edie in the mirror. 'He loves a girl with pluck,' she said pointedly.

Edie looked away.

'You're brave, Edith,' Miss Fotheringay had said to her once, when Edie had told her how with Babka she had learnt that it was better to keep her feelings back. But Aunt Sophia would never have understood. At Folly there were no marks awarded for holding back. Everyone was judged on whether they were prepared to do stupid things in the pouring rain.

And it was pouring by the time they reached Folly, where a bedraggled grey dog appeared to greet them as they got out of the car.

'Lyle's,' Aunt Sophia shuddered, stubbing out her cigarette on the steering wheel. 'Wretched creature. It howls all night.'

The dog slunk back into a doorway and watched, growling, as Edie and Janet carried their bags across the courtyard towards the house. Edie looked at the debris strewn about the porch – a tractor wheel, a fridge lying discarded beside an upturned quad bike, and noted with detached curiosity the unopened sacks of chicken feed piled by the front door. She guessed that Uncle Tony had gone away again, but thought better of enquiring.

As they followed Aunt Sophia into the freezing hallway, Edie stole a glance at Janet – regretful, but only half-apologetic, for after all, Edie had warned her not to come. But to Edie's fury Janet would not be drawn into the conspiracy, and went on talking to Aunt Sophia.

'I wish I'd brought my riding kit. Can you lend me any?' Then, 'Wow, how many dogs have you got?' she asked, dropping her bag to wrestle with a sopping Labrador.

Edie looked at her crossly. At school Janet was always so rude to the teachers that Edie sometimes found herself on the grown-ups' side, but here she seemed intent on ingratiating herself.

They followed Aunt Sophia to the kitchen, which was usually the only warm room in the house. But today the woodstove had not been lit and it struck Edie that the room was even more unkempt than usual, with the pig bucket overflowing beneath the sink, and the long table half-vanished beneath a tide of unwashed crockery. There was no sign of the late lunch the girls had been hoping for.

'I suppose you're starvacious,' Aunt Sophia said, looking around the room with a searching expression, as though expecting a meal suddenly to appear.

'Starvacious?' Janet sounded amused.

'Oh, sorry, darling, don't you lot use that word any more? I'm only trying to join in. But I'm so old I might as well be dead,' she said, turning with a theatrical grimace from the splintered mirror that hung beside the door.

Janet laughed: 'You look great! My mother says that it's the women who have all that stuff done – you know, face-lifts and everything, who age much quicker.'

Aunt Sophia seemed delighted – 'Oh, Juliet, you must come and stay again.'

Edie felt exasperated. Janet had always talked of her mother as if she despised her – but now she was quoting her as a fount of knowledge.

'Have some toast for now and I'll try and rustle up something for supper,' Aunt Sophia said, opening the fridge door, then slamming it in disgust. 'I'd better feed the animals first. And I suppose Juliet here will want to know where she's sleeping,' she said, as though the thought had suddenly struck her.

'She can come in with me,' Edie said firmly.

'Good idea,' said Aunt Sophia. 'I forgot you had an extra bed. Take some clean sheets from the airing cupboard on your way up, why don't you?'

Edie seized the opportunity to steer Janet upstairs, trying to distract her attention from the precarious piles of junk – trunks and bits of furniture, a stained bath – lying abandoned on the landing.

'Wow! Look at these!' Janet exclaimed, pausing to peer at two dead foxes in a glass cage.

'I've looked,' Edie said. She found something staged in Janet's enthusiasm, and wondered whether she was putting it on to annoy her. 'You should have brought a sleeping bag with you, the sheets here are always damp,' she added dismally. But when Edie opened the door to the airing cupboard she forgot about sheets in her fright at the two grimy faces peering up at her from the bottom shelf.

'Hullo, coz,' said Jason, flashing up his torch from where he lay, his head touching his twin's. 'We're hiding from Lyle. Don't tell him, will you? Promise!'

'She won't tell,' said Tom. 'She hates him even more than she hates us. Go away, Edie, please – buzz off and close the door.'

'Hey!' said Janet. 'Don't be so rude! For all you know, Edie might have decided to stop hating you.'

'Oh yeah,' said Jason. 'Sounds like you don't know her very well.'

'She despises us,' added Tom.

Janet looked at Edie, one eyebrow raised in mock interrogation. 'Well, Edie? To hate, or not to hate. Do you?' Then, 'Oh no, how could anyone hate you?' she cooed, leaning down to pat Jason on the head as though he were a dog. 'I'd like to take you back to school and keep you on my pillow, tucked up with the teddy bears!'

'Eugh, get off me!' Jason cried, recoiling with a squeal.

Edie looked at Janet with grudging admiration. Then – 'We need some sheets,' she said shortly, refusing to play Janet's game.

As they made their way upstairs, Janet kept stopping to tap on the walls. 'There might be secret passages,' she explained, with glinting eyes. 'This is just the sort of old house where you find them.'

'What's come over you?' Edie asked. 'This isn't the Famous Five.'

Then when they reached Edie's bedroom, Janet let out a gasp of pleasure. 'Oh, Edie, this place is cool,' she said, taking in the sloping attic room with its yellowed basin and peeling wallpaper, and the fireplace scattered with bird droppings. 'And it's so remote,' she went on, peering from the window into the rain.

Edie shrugged. She hated the remoteness at Folly Farm, and at the sight of the cracked window-pane and the stained mattresses she felt a familiar unease descend.

'I'm sorry that Aunt Sophia keeps calling you Juliet,' she said.

'Relax, Edie. I'm used to answering to lots of names – even my father never calls me Janet. I like it here.'

'Please don't like it too much,' Edie said, 'or I won't be able to like you.' Then, 'Wh-what's the matter?' she stammered, as Janet spun round with a furious face.

But Janet turned away again, shaking her head. 'I don't like being told what to feel,' she said finally, speaking with her head leant towards the window. 'It's what my parents do. Whichever one of them I'm with, they're always down on the other and I can't bear it.'

'I'm s-sorry,' Edie said, taken aback.

'At least now my mother's in America so I don't have

to see her so much – thank God,' Janet said bitterly.

'And what about your father?' Edie said, for she had noticed that Janet never talked about him.

Janet glowered. 'He's toast,' she said vehemently.

'Why, what's he done?'

'What's he not done, more like!' Janet was silent for a moment, then spoke in a bitter rush: 'I've always defended him to Mum. She's always gone on about how useless he is, just because he likes a drink and he doesn't care about what she cares about – fashion and money and all that rubbish! I've always told her to leave him alone and let us be – but then suddenly she got this job in New York, and she made him agree to send me to your stupid school. I told him I didn't want to come. All my life I've stuck up for him – but would he stick up for me? No he would *not*! He was pathetic! He thinks he should be able to see me because he lives near the school, but he's wrong. I'm cutting him out of my life!'

'That must be awful,' said Edie uncertainly. 'I mean, to be so angry with them. How – how long have they been divorced?'

Janet looked at her mockingly. 'Who said anything about marriage?'

'Sorry,' said Edie again, and blushed.

'You are positively rectangular sometimes, Wilson. Do you actually have any idea how babies are made?'

'Don't be stupid. Of course I do.'

'Of course you do,' Janet agreed. 'But you wouldn't if you knew my parents. It's unimaginable. I mean, they can't even be in the same room.' She shook her head in a show of horror.

'What I don't get,' said Edie into an embarrassed silence, 'is why you're so desperate to leave school when you hate home. If you succeed in getting chucked out of Knight's Haddon, you'll have to live with one of them. Wouldn't that be worse?' She was thinking of her own case, of her bad-tempered grandmother who had taught her at home, but who was now in a nursing home. School, for Edie, had been a lucky escape.

'Good point, Wilson. I used to worry about where I'd go next. But it's all right now.' Janet smiled mysteriously. 'I've got a plan.'

'What sort of plan?' Edie asked.

Janet looked at her hesitantly a moment, as if weighing something up. 'Later,' she said, with sudden resolution as she seized her duffel coat from the bed. 'Come on, I'm starving, let's go and teach your aunt how to cook.'

History Revisited

Edie was unsettled by Janet's outburst. But for all her talk of rebellion, Folly seemed to have transformed her into a model child, lavishing charm on everyone. She even seemed determined to get on with Uncle Tony's foul-breathed barrel of a spaniel, who soon started following her faithfully.

'Hello, Lancelot,' Janet crooned, as she stooped to nuzzle its ears. 'Poor, stinking old thing,' she added playfully, holding her nose. 'No wonder no one lets you sleep on their bed!' The dog wriggled in delight, and rewarded Janet with a slobbering kiss on the chin.

'I didn't know you liked dogs,' Edie said.

'I like this one,' Janet replied.

'I don't like any of the Folly dogs, but one term last year Matron came back to school with this silver whippet she was looking after, and I—'

'Stop!' said Janet, pressing her hands to her ears as she followed Edie into the kitchen. 'I am determined not to think about that place until we are back inside the prison walls.'

Edie felt flattened – then gave a start when she saw Lyle looking up at her from the easy chair beside the stove, where he sat with his legs sprawled, a sneering look on his face.

'Hello, coz. Aren't you going to introduce me to your friend?'

'I'm Janet,' said Janet. 'Is that introduction enough?'

'Oh God,' said Aunt Sophia, speaking into the fridge. 'Did I call you something else? I'm useless with names. And that reminds me,' she said, turning round with a chicken carcass clasped to her breast, 'Juliet here – I mean, Jane—'

'Janet, Soph. Her name is Janet, get a grip,' said Lyle.

'It doesn't matter what her name is,' Aunt Sophia snapped. 'The point is, she'd like to ride. I hoped Tony would take her out but he's just rung to say he won't be back this weekend.'

Jason and Tom looked up from their computer game in protest:

'But he promised—'

'He's never here—'

'He said—'

'So what do you want me to do about it?' Aunt Sophia replied, slamming the fridge door with her foot. 'Oh, darling, you'll have to take us as you find us,' she went on, addressing Janet in a feeble tone. 'I expect Edie's told you about her uncle Tony. He's very committed to . . . changing the world. Back to what it used to be. He thinks we should all live on the land – you know, self-sufficiency. Eggs for breakfast, nettle soup for supper—' Aunt Sophia waved a wooden spoon around the kitchen, as if to demonstrate how the system worked. 'And he's so busy spreading the message that he's never here to live the dream.'

'Which is in fact a nightmare,' said Tom.

Janet cocked her head politely. Edie had told her nothing about Uncle Tony, except that he wasn't often there.

Eventually supper appeared on the table – charred baked potatoes and some scraps of cold chicken.

'Jason! Tom! Chop chop! Knives and forks!' Aunt Sophia said, swatting Lyle's hand from the wine bottle.

'Why not Lyle?' asked Jason.

'Why not Edie?' said Tom.

'Why not Janet?' said Lyle.

'Shut up, all of you, and sit down!' Aunt Sophia shouted, collapsing into a chair. 'Sorry about supper,' she added, to no one in particular. 'I was going to make a risotto, but trouble is that these things' – she waved her cigarette in the air – 'have destroyed my taste buds. And that makes cooking so much harder.'

'Who's this?' Lyle said, pointing at the chicken plate.

'Henny Penny,' Aunt Sophia sighed. 'Poor dear. But she's fed us well.'

Lyle and Jason smirked, but Edie felt a revolt in her

stomach. It was one of the hateful rituals at Folly Farm, that all the chickens were given silly names before being slaughtered – so that at mealtimes the identity of each bird could be announced with relish.

Once Jason had told Edie that when Uncle Tony went away it was Lyle who did the killing, and an image came to her now, of Lyle in a dark barn, smiling crookedly as he closed his hands round Henny Penny's neck. She pushed away her plate.

'Oh God, darling, I'm sorry, I've put you off your food,' Aunt Sophia said. 'You mustn't be squeamish. If it wasn't for those mangy old birds – oh, God knows, the hens stand between us and the pig bucket.'

Edie hoped that at least Janet would now understand why she hated Folly so much. But when she glanced at her friend for sympathy, she received none in return.

'Come on, Edie. You love chicken. Don't be like Anastasia.'

'What's Anastasia like?' asked Aunt Sophia, suddenly interested. 'We haven't been allowed to meet her,' she added, pulling a doleful face.

Edie said nothing. She and Anastasia might have fallen out, but something in Aunt Sophia's glib tone made her feel fiercely protective.

'She's soppy,' Janet volunteered. 'And tyrannical.'

'Fascinating,' said Aunt Sophia. 'Sounds like Hitler.'

'No!' Edie protested. 'Anastasia is not like Hitler!'

'Ssh, darling, don't take it personally. It is an interesting historical fact that dictators are always soppy about animals. Hitler and Mussolini were both mass murderers *and* vegetarians.'

'What about Stalin?' asked Janet.

'Stalin, admittedly, was the exception,' said Aunt Sophia. 'Someone told me he once lost his temper with a budgerigar, and cracked open its skull with his pipe.'

Lyle whistled. 'What had it done?'

Aunt Sophia shrugged. 'Sung.'

'Yea!' said Lyle. 'Stalin's my man.'

The others laughed. Except for Edie. Babka had told her about Stalin. He wasn't a joke. He was evil. No wonder Lyle admired him!

'Talking of dictators,' Aunt Sophia said sweetly, 'how is the headmistress of Knight's Haddon?'

'Do you know her?' asked Janet, making a face.

'Oh God, do I know Caro Foth–er–in–gay,' Aunt Sophia drawled in answer. 'Yes – and no. I know her, but I don't get her. Are you still mad about her, darling?' she asked Edie, blowing a smoke ring in her direction.

The boys sniggered.

'Crazy about her, Edie, aren't you?' Janet teased.

Then – 'Sulking?' Lyle called, as Edie got up from the table.

Edie turned on the television in the sitting room to drown out the laughter from next door. There was no reception in the valley, just a DVD player for which the boys had a small stock of films they watched over and over again. She pressed 'play' and was not surprised to see a gun going off. It was a war film. She sat and watched, barely concentrating at first, determined only to ignore the sounds of laughter coming from the kitchen, but gradually the rhythmic monotony of death and uniforms started to absorb her, and she hardly noticed when the twins came and stood behind the sofa. An elderly German prisoner had just been smuggled out from a prison called Spandau, but he was not responding as happily as his rescuers seemed to expect.

'I didn't know you liked war films, Edie,' said Aunt Sophia, appearing briefly in the doorway.

'I vant to go home, and my home is Spandau,' the German said.

Jason smirked.

'I feel sorry for him,' Edie said bitterly.

'You do know he's a Nazi?' Jason said.

Edie hadn't. 'So what?' she said.

'Edie is a Nazi, Edie is a Nazi, Nazi, Nazi, Nazi,' Jason began to shout gleefully.

'*Shut* up!'

'Nazi, Nazi, Nazi!' Tom joined in.

'Edie vants to go home and her home is Knight's Haddon,' Lyle jeered, with unusual perception, as she walked out in disgust.

She was in bed, but still awake, when Janet appeared an hour later and flung a hard metal object into her suitcase.

'What's that?' Edie asked sullenly. 'It looks like a murder weapon.'

'A bicycle lock. Lyle gave it to me.'

'What for?'

'Er – like, try locking up bicycles,' Janet replied.

'But you don't have a bicycle.'

'No. But I've got a bicycle lock. Anyway, what happened to you?' she said.

'You saw what happened,' Edie said furiously. 'It was called Lyle.'

'He's not so bad,' Janet said, standing at the sink. 'At least he's funny.'

'No he's not. He's stupid, and mean.'

Janet shrugged. 'We're all stupid and mean sometimes,' she said.

'Rubbish!' Edie replied, her voice shaking. 'I'm not! And I thought, before tonight, that you weren't either! Whenever you complain about your mother, I've always taken your side. How would you feel if I came home on an *exeat* with you, and ganged up with her at your expense! Well, that's what it feels like now!'

Janet put down her toothbrush with a sigh. 'Listen, Edie, all I'm saying is that there are always two sides. Yes, I know it's boring, I know it's what grown-ups say, but it's also true. You have a story about your cousins. They have a story about you. It's not the same story – but you can see how it joins up.'

'What do you mean?' Edie asked, outraged. 'How do you know? Have you been talking to them about me?'

'Don't go mad,' Janet said. 'I didn't start the conversation.'

'What did they say about me?' Edie demanded.

'They asked if I liked you, and I said that of course I did, and I asked why they didn't like you too – and they told me all about you coming to live here, and about you making it clear that you hated them all, and that you despised them for being country cousins who didn't read books, and that you never wanted to join in but just sat by the pond moping and talking to a fish.'

Edie burned at the injustice of it. 'Did they tell you what happened to the fish?'

'No, what happened?' Janet said.

'They caught her, and they cooked her, and they tried to make me eat her,' Edie said in a low, trembling voice.

Janet frowned, and chewed her lip. Then to Edie's disbelief she started laughing. 'OK, OK, it's horrid,' Janet spluttered, giving up all attempt at control. 'But . . . oh God, Edie, you've . . . you've got to admit it . . . it *is* quite funny!'

When Edie woke up next morning, Janet had gone. Edie knew she must have got up early to go out riding with Lyle, and stared at the deserted bed in a sullen fury, cursing that she had ever agreed to let her come.

She wondered how long Janet would be away, wondered if she would come upstairs looking for her when she got back, muddied and apologetic – or if she would notice if Edie never appeared; she wondered, bitterly, if any of them would even come upstairs to check if she were alive or dead. Edie thought of putting it to the test by staying in bed all day.

But hunger and boredom eventually drove her downstairs to the deserted kitchen. The dishes from an earlier breakfast still lay strewn on the table – the food was gone, but Edie could tell from the greasy pans that Janet and Lyle had eaten well. She wondered where the meal had been magicked from, for when she looked in the fridge there was nothing but a few open tins of dog food and a bag of stale bread. She found some ginger biscuits, and poured herself the cold dregs of tea from the pot, thinking longingly of the breakfast buffet at Knight's Haddon, with the tubs of cereals lined up on the counter, labelled with copper discs, the shining tea urn and the loaves of hot bread.

She was sitting at the table, making a desolate attempt at her weekend homework, when Aunt Sophia wandered in and slung a dead chicken on the table.

'Hello, darling. What are you doing?'

'Homework,' Edie said drily.

'Oh dear,' Aunt Sophia replied, with a harassed glance at the pile of books. 'Why don't you stay in bed until lunch time, like normal teenagers do?'

'Er, maybe because I'm not a teenager – yet,' Edie replied.

Sophia threw her a suspicious look. 'Aren't you? Christ, how time does drag. Did you have – is there any – breakfast?'

'Biscuits and cold tea with no milk,' Edie said glumly. 'There wasn't anything else.'

'Edie darling, don't sulk. What's wrong with making your own tea? Someone's been cooking anyway,' Aunt Sophia went on, peering into the remains of Lyle's fry-up. 'It's Lyle, I bet. That boy is like a drug dealer, always has a secret supply even when the rest of us are starving to death.'

'If Lyle can get hold of food, then why can't you?' asked Jason, sidling into the room with an expression of growling hunger on his face.

'I try, I try,' Aunt Sophia whined. 'I'm always shopping, but you're always eating. I can't keep up.'

'Most mothers want their children to eat to make them grow,' said Tom, siding with his twin. 'But you wish we'd stayed little.'

'You were much nicer when you couldn't speak,' Aunt Sophia agreed. She looked at him, smiling, then seized by some sudden force of affection she reached from the chicken she had started plucking and playfully tweaked his ear.

'Ugh,' Jason shrieked, springing away in disgust.

Edie watched with a surge of jealousy. No one would ever tell her that they had loved her best when she was a baby; no one had ever loved her, no one at all. Her mother – Anna – hadn't wanted to be a mother; she had run off as soon as Edie was born. Miss Fotheringay's words rang back to her through a void of loneliness: *'Anna wrote to me and said that it was her life.'*

What about Edie's life? Why hadn't she counted? Did no one care?

'She can't hear you. She's gone into one of her dreams.'

'Wakey wakey, Edie. What's it about this time?'

'Most likely she's thanking her stars she doesn't have an embarrassing mother,' said Jason, wrinkling his nose.

Edie glared at him, sickened. She hated them all.

'That's a stupid thing to say, Jace,' Tom said quietly.

Edie looked at him gratefully. It was harder to hate

Tom than the others. He was the gentler of the twins – perhaps, Edie supposed, because Aunt Sophia had always favoured Jason. 'Mum likes a bit of rough,' Lyle had once said, leering. 'And Jason's rough as leather,' he'd added, chucking a bread pellet at his younger brother.

Tom had laughed. 'My time will come,' he'd said, sounding surprisingly grown-up, but there had been something plaintive in his voice, which Edie remembered now. Tom was an outsider too. His brothers called him 'the hairdresser', or just 'the girl', because even though he was only ten years old he already used hair gel, and hogged the bathroom.

But Tom was different from Edie; most of the time he seemed not to mind being teased.

'You're such a girl, why don't you join forces with Edie?' Jason said to him now, making a grab for the biscuit tin.

'Edie's not girl enough for me,' Tom shrugged. 'And nor's she!' he added, as Janet flung into the kitchen and collapsed with a groan of high spirits into a sagging chair.

'Take pity on me, please!' wailed Newgirl, stretching out her legs with a coquettish smile. 'These boots are a size too small! I need boy power to get them off.'

Edie watched with amazement as first one twin, then the other, rallied to either side of her and stood wrestling a boot each.

'One-two-three, *go*!' shouted Janet, shrieking with laughter as her boots flew off and the boys tumbled to the floor.

'Oh God, darling, you are a scream!' said Aunt Sophia, laughing, as Jason rolled into her.

A scream, Edie thought. *Janet is a scream, a joining-inning, giggle-making, mother-hating, cold-blooded scream, and I should be a scream too . . . but I can't, I can't, I CAN'T!*

And she snatched up her homework and walked into the television room with her mouth set in an angry line.

The Dressing Gown Clue

Edie hardly spoke to Janet on the train back to school. She was too angry. Janet might laugh at what Lyle had done to her fish, but Edie didn't see the joke.

And there had been something else between Janet and Lyle that Edie hadn't liked.

'I dare you!' Lyle had said that morning, when Edie and Janet had appeared in the kitchen.

'Dare me what?' Edie asked.

'Not you, coz, her,' Lyle had replied, nodding at Janet.

But when Edie had looked at Janet for an explanation, Janet had laughed it off.

Edie stared out of the train window, wondering what they had been plotting.

'What's up?' Janet asked, putting down her book.

'Nothing,' Edie lied, picking up hers.

Miss Pickering had sent a taxi to meet their train. Edie sat in the front, and when they reached the school she hurried inside while Janet was still unloading her bags.

It was nearly bedtime, but Edie couldn't face going back to her dormitory in the South Tower, and being cold-shouldered by everyone. Janet had been her only ally since the ferrets escaped – but after their disastrous weekend together, Edie supposed she would now have no one to speak to at all.

Most of all she dreaded seeing Anastasia, and hearing her show off about her *exeat* with Fothy. Edie imagined her sitting on the headmistress's sofa, Black Puss purring by her side, and she felt furious and miserable. Anastasia won everyone round in the end.

Edie let herself into the library and slammed the door. The room was dark, and here at least she could be alone. But as she was fumbling for the light switch she heard a noise that made her jump.

Then: 'There you are!' came a voice, and as the lights came on she saw Anastasia looking up at her from a desk.

'Anastasia, what are you doing sitting here in the dark?' Edie asked, wondering if she was in for another attack.

But Anastasia's manner was awkward. 'Thought you might come here,' she said, standing up and smiling at Edie shyly. 'How was your weekend?'

'Awful,' Edie said. 'You were right about Janet. She's—' Then – 'Oh, what's it matter?' she said impatiently, remembering that she and Anastasia were enemies too.

But Anastasia rushed up and flung her arms round Edie's neck. 'Oh, Edie, thank goodness!' she cried, clasping her tight. 'I was terrified you'd have come back best friends with her, and then you wouldn't believe me!'

'Believe what?' Edie said, alarmed by this sudden embrace.

'What I should have seen all along,' Anastasia said, moving back and looking at her friend solemnly. 'Oh, Edie, I owe you an apology. I know now it wasn't you!'

'But – how . . .' Edie shook her head, bewildered.

'The dressing gown, of course. I don't know how I could have been so stupid, not to have worked it out before—'

'The dressing gown?' Edie said stupidly.

'Oh, Edie, don't you see!' Anastasia squeezed Edie's hands in hers, talking in an excited rush. 'It was Janet! It was Janet who let the ferrets go! She's the one who sneaked out to the animal house in the middle of the night and set them free – and she was wearing your dressing gown!'

'But what's my dressing gown got to do with it?' Edie asked, still lost.

Anastasia smiled at her apologetically. 'Oh, Edie, I'm so ashamed by how much I didn't tell you.' She steered Edie into a chair, and sat opposite her, leaning forward and talking in a hurried whisper, as if fearing Janet might be lurking behind one of the library shelves. 'That night, Edie, the night I accused you of having let the ferrets go . . . well, Matron found your dressing gown with mud on it and took it away to get it washed! We all suspected you anyway of course, but that seemed to prove it! Your dressing gown, muddied from the scene of the crime!'

Edie was stunned. She hardly ever wore her dressing gown, and hadn't even noticed that it had been washed. 'But why – why didn't . . . ?' she began.

Anastasia looked ashamed. 'We, we would have told you, Edie – but somehow—'

Edie shook her head, struggling to comprehend it. 'But Alice, and Sally – why didn't they say something? If you all thought the dressing gown was proof that I'd done it, then why didn't you confront me instead of just' – Edie thought of what she had suffered and looked at Anastasia with a rush of rage – 'instead of all condemning me without a trial!'

'Don't blame the others, Edie. It was all my fault. I told them you did it and I know some of them didn't believe it at first, certainly not Alice, but when Matron found your dressing gown covered in mud, everyone agreed that it had to have been you.'

'OK,' Edie said, her voice expressionless. 'So how does Janet come into it?'

Anastasia leant forward, and seized Edie's hand. 'It was during fire drill that I realized I'd got it all wrong,' she whispered fervently. 'When I saw Janet wearing your dressing gown everything made sense, Edie! I mean, of course you wouldn't have worn your dressing gown to go out to the animal house in the middle of the night – it's so long, and you can't walk in it without tripping over. But it's not too long for Janet! She can even do cartwheels in it!'

'Steady,' Edie said. 'We don't know for sure—'

'We do!' Anastasia said passionately. 'And Janet doesn't have her own dressing gown! That's why she borrowed yours, remember? I'm so sorry, Edie . . . I – I don't think I've ever been so sorry for anything in my life, ever.'

Anastasia looked at her tearfully, but it was Janet's face that Edie saw, as threads of their mysterious conversations came flashing back:

'What people don't know can't hurt them . . . I'm afraid to tell you stuff, and that's not because I don't like you, it's because I do . . .'

'I would have called you over the weekend,' Anastasia rushed on. 'But I was frightened you'd tell Janet, and that she'd persuade you it wasn't her – when I know that it was! Oh, Edie, how could I ever have accused you! It was all my fault! If I hadn't been so sure about it, everyone would have given you a chance!'

Edie shook her head. She felt overwhelmed.

'But – but, Edie, why didn't you stick up for yourself? If only you'd made more of a fuss, and told me what an idiot I was being, then I might have worked it out sooner!'

'You didn't give me much chance to explain myself,' Edie said. But she felt no anger now. Anastasia's remorse seemed more sincere than her wild accusations had ever been – and Edie felt all her hurt extinguished by a wave of relief.

They sat in silence a moment, as if struck by a brief awkwardness at becoming friends again.

'Edie,' Anastasia said. 'If I tell you something really, *really* despicable – do you think you'll ever forgive me?'

'Depends what it is,' Edie said, smiling.

Anastasia looked hesitant. 'I know everyone's going to hate me, Edie, when they find out it's Papa who's bought the tower – to build a house for mummy. They'll all turn against me, and say it's my fault that the school can't use the stupid tower any more. I could see it coming, Edie, how horrid it would be with everyone turning against me, just like – just like they did in my first term!'

Edie shook her head. It was true that Anastasia had been distrusted when she had first come to Knight's Haddon, but that had been due to one of the mistresses undermining her – and once the plot had been exposed, everyone had rallied to Anastasia's defence.

'No one's going to blame you for the tower, Anastasia,' Edie began. 'When they know the truth, they'll all understand.'

'They *will* blame me!' Anastasia said bitterly. 'They'll think I'm a spoilt princess getting my own fairy-tale tower in the woods, and—' Her voice faltered. 'Oh, Edie, it's so awful – but I thought how much they'd all hate me, and part of me wanted you to be unpopular too! Oh God, it's so shameful, I hardly know what I'm saying!'

Edie suddenly laughed. 'It might have been quite fun, being the Two Most Unpopular Girls in the School,' she said.

Anastasia smiled. 'I don't deserve you as a friend, Edie,' she said.

Edie was silent a moment, remembering that Janet had said the same thing.

'But did you really think I let the ferrets go?' she asked suddenly.

Anastasia turned crimson. 'I don't know what I thought, Edie. I was so jealous of you and Janet being friends that I'd have convinced myself of anything. But to think that it was Janet all along!'

'We've no proof it was Janet,' Edie said slowly. 'I mean, what would her motive be?'

'Spite,' Anastasia said darkly. 'She wanted to break us up so she could have you all to herself – and she very nearly did it!'

'But she liked the ferrets,' Edie said.

Anastasia shrugged. 'That doesn't mean she didn't do it! She probably thought they'd be happier free.'

Edie nodded thoughtfully, remembering what Janet had said to her at breakfast. '*They'll be fine . . . they belong in the wild . . .*'

'But if it was her,' Edie said cautiously, 'and if she did wear my dressing gown when she did it, wouldn't it be a bit odd of her to wear it again during the fire drill, when everyone could see?'

Anastasia waved Edie's reservations aside: 'Criminals love taking risks – like murderers who keep returning to the scene of the crime! Come on, Edie, we know it was her! And when I've finished with her, she'll—'

'No!' Edie said suddenly. 'You got it wrong before,

Anastasia, and this time you're going to listen to me. Don't say anything about this – nothing at all.'

Anastasia looked startled. 'What do you mean? We can't go on letting the rest of the school think it was you.'

'We won't – at least, not for long. But Janet's up to something, Anastasia, and I want to find out what it is before we let on that we've rumbled her.'

'Up to what?'

'That's the whole point, idiot – I don't know.' Then Edie told Anastasia how she thought Janet was hiding something from her, and described how Newgirl had snuck out on her own one weekend. And as she spoke she remembered what she had overheard about food going missing from the school kitchens. Could Janet be involved in that too?

'But what would she do with raw eggs and sausages?'

'Search me,' Edie said. 'But if you promise not to rush in and accuse her about the ferrets, we might find out.'

Anastasia looked intrigued.

'So, Detective Stolonov – in or out?' Edie asked.

'In,' Anastasia agreed.

KNIGHT'S HADDON

A Key Without a Lock

Janet was already in bed when Edie returned to the dormitory.

'Sweet?' Janet offered, thrusting a bag of strawberry shoelaces from under her covers.

Edie ignored her, and when she got into bed she lay facing the other way. But her eyes kept moving to the mocking red dressing gown hanging on the dormitory door. She heard an echo of the pep talk Cousin Charles had given her a year ago, when he had delivered her to Knight's Haddon to act as Prince Stolonov's schoolgirl spy:

'Remember everything, Edith, never let anything go: most mysteries are solved by attention to the most trivial-seeming details . . . all you'll need are your eyes and ears.'

Edie imagined how scornful Cousin Charles would be

of her inattentiveness now.

She and Anastasia would prove who the real culprit was! But an instinct told Edie they shouldn't confront Janet too hastily. She was in little doubt now that Janet had done it – it made sense of all her riddles about secrecy. But she still wondered at Newgirl's motive, when the ferrets had clearly given her so much pleasure. Even if they could make Janet confess to having let the ferrets go, the story didn't feel complete.

Janet had other secrets, Edie felt sure of it. She listened to her snoring in the next door bed, and wondered what mischief she was plotting.

For the next few days she and Anastasia were joined in duplicity, keeping all their suspicions under wraps. Edie reflected that it had been almost worth falling out with Anastasia for the pleasure of making up with her again. They plunged back into their best-friendship with new vigour, as if wanting to seize back all the precious days they'd lost.

But the other girls, who still assumed Edie guilty, were bewildered to the see the friendship back on track.

'Don't you see, Anastasia had to forgive her,' Edie overheard Phoebe explaining to Rose by the wash basins one night. 'Edie's like her handmaiden, she does every-thing for her. She probably even polishes her shoes when we're not looking. I knew Anastasia wouldn't last long without her.'

Edie listened with scorn. Phoebe had never had a best friend – no wonder she was jealous. 'Edie the Liberator',

Phoebe had christened her when the ferrets had gone, but now it was 'Edie the slave'.

As for Janet, she lost no opportunity to snipe. 'I'm so glad Princess Ansti's won you back,' she said sneeringly, as Edie was changing into her pyjamas one night. 'I was thinking we'd have to send off to Russia for a replacement maid. Chop chop!' she chided, as the bedtime bell rang out. 'She'll need her sheets turned down and her hot water-bottle filled and her pillow plumped, and dear me,' Janet went on playfully, checking her watch, 'have you ironed her nightie and folded away her clothes?'

'Oh, buzz off and change the record, why don't you?' Edie said, flinging herself on the bed, and picking up her book.

Anastasia hated to see Edie still in the dock. 'When can we confront her, Edie?' she asked impatiently. 'Until we do, everyone will go on thinking it was you! Can't I at least tell them that I know it wasn't?'

Edie shrugged. 'Another few days in Coventry won't kill me. It's beginning to feel quite like home.' She was convinced that Janet would reveal something, sooner or later.

And so she did. It was during lunch break, on the Wednesday after the *exeat*, and Edie and Anastasia had just entered the hall, where the day's letters and parcels were laid out each afternoon on a long trestle table. It was Matron's job to sort through the post, and weed out any packages containing mobile phones, or illicit supplies of sweets. Some of the girls despaired of her sniffer-dog instincts – 'Fothy's private bloodhound',

Sally called her – but Edie wasn't bothered. No one ever sent parcels to her.

She hung back as the other girls stampeded eagerly to the table.

'A letter from Papa!' Anastasia said, clutching an envelope as she ducked out of the crowd. She tore it open immediately, reading it as if in a world of her own, seemingly oblivious to the girls jostling past her to reach the table. Edie smiled. She guessed from Anastasia's delighted expression that her disgrace over the trip to the horse fair was forgiven.

When Edie checked the table, there was nothing addressed to her. But then she saw a letter that caught her eye. It was the semi-literate handwriting on the envelope that struck her, the letters jagged and mis-shapen, barely joined up – Edie recognized it at once as Lyle's. But the letter was addressed to Janet.

An excitement shot through her. Why had he written to her? What if he had mentioned the ferrets in the let-ter? Even some coded reference to them would be enough for Edie to seize on. She looked at the letter furtively, and before she quite knew what she was doing she had slipped it into the pocket of her skirt.

'Edie!' Anastasia said, running up to her excitedly. 'Papa's asked if you can come to France for Easter – back to Menton! Oh, Edie, will you come? Will you?'

'Will I?' Edie laughed, catching her breath as Anasta-sia clutched her shoulders and hoisted her around the hall in a wild dance. They had just collided with a first year when Edie saw Janet appear. 'Come on!' she said, pulling herself free. 'We'll be late.'

Anastasia was thrilled with the holiday plans. She talked of her father's French cook all through lunch, while eating her toad-in-the-hole with zeal.

But Edie was barely listening. Her thoughts kept returning guiltily to the stolen letter in her pocket. She wondered if she should tell Anastasia, but something warned her against it. If the letter contained the proof they needed, Edie wanted to uncover it first, before getting Anastasia's hopes up.

It wasn't until the short break during afternoon lessons that she had a chance to slip into the cloakroom on her own, and see what it said.

The envelope was thick, and when Edie opened it she found something padded in tissue paper. She looked at it suspiciously, wondering if it might be one of Lyle's practical jokes, but when she pulled the tissue paper away she saw a postcard of a pig. And on the back of it, attached with sellotape, was a small silver key.

To her disappointment there was no writing at all.

Edie examined the key curiously, wondering what it could be. It looked as if it would fit a padlock – but for what? It was one of Miss Fotheringay's rules that nothing could be locked. Then she remembered the bicycle padlock. But what did Janet need to lock up?

'Edie, hi! What are you doing in here?'

Edie looked up with a jolt to see Sally staring at her curiously. 'Nothing,' she mumbled, stuffing the postcard back into the envelope.

She made her way to the classroom, calculating fast.

Janet was up to something, and if Edie could only find out what the key was for, things might finally start to make sense. The first thing was to return the letter, then to find out what she did with the lock and key. But Janet must never suspect that her letter had been intercepted.

Edie looked at her watch. She still had five minutes until lessons began. She hurried on to the classroom, and re-sealed the envelope with glue, then tucked the letter back in her pocket and darted towards the hall.

The other girls were already making their way towards their classrooms, and the hall was deserted when Edie arrived. She walked up to the table and saw to her relief that several letters had still to be collected – she could slip Janet's back among them; no one would notice a thing.

She glanced over her shoulder, then took the letter from her pocket, feeling a guilty satisfaction. She had been wrongly blamed for releasing the ferrets, so it seemed fair enough that her real crime should go un-detected.

But as Edie was slipping the letter back into the pile, she heard a voice behind her shoulder and spun round to see Miss Fotheringay watching her closely.

'What are you up to now, Edith Wilson?' the head-mistress asked, with a smile.

'Nothing,' Edie said, blushing.

Deeds, Not Words

Edie felt uncomfortable all afternoon. *'What are you up to now, Edith Wilson?'* Nothing ever escaped Miss Fotheringay – she would surely have guessed that Edie had been reading Janet's post. Edie remembered how cross she had been at the beginning of term, when Fothy had seemed to want her to spy on Janet. But now she had fallen into the trap, and she could imagine what Phoebe and the others would say if they found out what she'd done: *'Watch out for Edie! She never gets any letters of her own, so she reads ours instead!'*

Anastasia, however, was fully on side. 'Brilliant bit of sleuthing,' she whispered admiringly, when Edie told her the story during tea.

'I don't *know* it's the key to the bicycle lock that she got at Folly,' Edie explained. 'But it would sort of make sense—'

'It must be!' Anastasia said, throwing Janet a sly glance down the table. 'But what's she going to do with it? She must have a bike she's planning to run away on.'

'But where's she hiding it?' Edie said. No one had a bicycle at Knight's Haddon.

'I don't know, but we've got to find out!' Anastasia said excitedly. 'Oh God, Edie – I wish we could just confront her, and force everything out. What are we waiting for? Let's take her somewhere secret and keep her there until she tells us the truth!'

Edie smiled. 'You mean, throw her into a dungeon and torture her into confessing?'

'Yes!' Anastasia said, imagining the scene with glee: *Janet Stone! Did you release Anastasia's ferrets? Was it you who raided the kitchens? And what is the meaning of this mysterious key? Have you got a bicycle? And if so, where is it? And where are you planning to go?* Oh, come on, Edie, I'm bored of spying. Let's put it to her, and see how she reacts!'

Edie was tempted. She was getting impatient too. But something told her they should bide their time. And meanwhile there was double history to get through.

Janet was for once already at her desk when Edie and Anastasia arrived in the classroom. But Edie was more surprised to see Miss Fotheringay standing on the raised dais at the front of the room.

'Sit down, girls, you're late,' the headmistress said crisply, looking up from her book. 'There is no need to look so startled, Anastasia. Miss Mannering has lost her voice so I am here to pick up where she left off. Perhaps someone would be so kind as to tell me where, exactly, that is.'

The class was silent. Edie stared uneasily into her notebook. Miss Fotheringay's lessons always had to melt before they could flow, and it struck Edie that this morning the atmosphere in the room was unusually icy.

'Sally, let's start with you.' The headmistress sounded a touch impatient. 'What are you learning about this term?'

'Suff-suffrage?' said Sally, looking uncertain.

Miss Fotheringay nodded. 'Suffrage history,' she said slowly, chalking the word on the board. 'The fight for the vote. And who can tell me where the word suffrage comes from?'

Silence, again.

'Edith?'

Edie clenched her hands under her desk. The fact that she knew the answer only made it worse: couldn't Miss Fotheringay see how the others teased her for being a teacher's pet? She thought of making up a wrong answer, but something in Miss Fotheringay's expression checked her. 'Latin . . . *suffragium*,' she murmured reluctantly.

'Very good,' Miss Fotheringay said.

'And what English words besides "suffrage" derive from *suffragium*?' Edie was relieved to see the headmistress's eyes roving the room for a new victim. 'Janet?'

Janet did not reply. First she tipped back her chair then she fell to fiddling with her glasses.

'Are your spectacles broken?' asked Miss Fotheringay. No answer.

'The loss of one sense is supposed to sharpen all the others, but Janet's temporary blindness seems to have affected her hearing.'

The class tittered nervously, but when Janet finally looked up her expression was blank.

'Your glasses,' hissed Edie, who was sitting next to her, and supposed Janet hadn't understood. 'Is there something wrong with them?'

'Oh,' said Janet. Then, 'No-o,' she replied in a mocking voice.

'Good,' Miss Fotheringay said coldly. 'Put them on then, and answer my question. Suffrage, as I am sure you know, means the right to vote. Can you give me words in English with the same root?'

Several hands were now raised, but Janet continued to slouch. 'Words?' she queried, in a bored voice.

'Yes, Janet. At Knight's Haddon we always look at the roots of words, followed by their branches. We see language as a tree.'

Janet looked profoundly uninterested.

'Do you know what we call the women who fought for the vote before the First World War, Janet?' Miss Fotheringay persevered.

'Yes,' said Janet. 'Of course I know.'

Miss Fotheringay gave a hint of interest. 'Then perhaps you would care to share this information with the class.'

Janet said nothing.

'If you know the answer, Janet, then why don't you say?'

'Deeds, not words,' Janet murmured, staring at the floor. Her voice was low, but the headmistress seized on what she'd said with twitching lips. 'Ah-ha! Did everyone hear that? *Deeds, not words*,' she then repeated triumphantly, tossing her chalk in the air. 'And that is a slogan popularized by the . . . ?'

'Suffragettes,' said Belinda.

'Correct,' Miss Fotheringay replied. 'The suffragettes was the name given to the women who appeared at political meetings at the beginning of the last century demanding one basic right. What was it? Edith?'

'They wanted women to be allowed to vote at general elections,' Edie replied cautiously.

'Excellent. I see Miss Mannering has taught you well. And can anyone tell me how they made themselves heard? Rose?'

'Did some of them tie themselves to the railings of the Houses of Parliament?'

Miss Fotheringay nodded. 'Eventually, yes. When their demands were ignored, they resorted to ever more extravagant gestures. But still no one listened, except to say what a nuisance they were.'

'Why didn't the government just let them vote?' asked a voice from the back of the class.

Miss Fotheringay frowned. 'Did that voice have a hand? I didn't see it.'

'Perhaps the voice belonged to a suffragette,' suggested Janet, whose voice was also without a hand.

Miss Fotheringay turned on her sharply. 'Not a bad joke, Janet, as jokes go, but as jokes go it's over. I wonder if *you* see yourself as something of a suffragette?'

Janet flushed. 'What's wrong with the suffragettes?'

Miss Fotheringay stood very still, staring at her implacably. 'I might as well ask you that question, Janet Stone. What was the result of disrupting political meetings? What did Emily Davison gain by throwing herself under the King's horse? Certainly not the right to vote: that was won years later, after the war. All the suffragettes achieved was getting women banned from political meetings. It is the usual story with extremists.'

Janet sat up abruptly and Edie looked at her in surprise. Newgirl's expression had hardened, and her eyes had a sudden zeal.

'Yes, Janet? Is there something you would like to contribute?'

'Yeah, all right. If you want me to.'

Miss Fotheringay inclined her head.

'I've – I've been reading a book . . .' Janet said.

'Excellent.'

If Janet detected the sarcasm in the headmistress's tone she gave no sign of it. She was frowning and stammering in contrast to her usual drawl. 'It's about the suffragettes . . . and, well, like, I—'

'Like?' queried Miss Fotheringay, holding up a hand to interrupt her. 'Who is like what in that sentence?'

'Eh?'

'Try and do without filler words, Janet. One of our little rules at Knight's Haddon. You have been reading a book about the suffragettes?'

Edie winced at Miss Fotheringay's taunting tone. Could she not see that Janet had something she felt it important to say?

'Yes,' said Janet, glowering. 'That's what I said.'

'And what have you learnt from your book?'

'Well,' said Janet. 'If the suffragettes hadn't kicked off like they did who knows when women would of got the vote.'

'Would have,' Miss Fotheringay corrected her. 'Subjunctive imperative.'

Janet flushed.

'It is, as you say, unknowable,' Miss Fotheringay went on merrily, with another hurl of her chalk into the air. 'But what we do know is that the vote was given to women after the First World War, when the suffragettes were no longer in existence. They were a revolutionary movement which fizzled out. The fact that history later caught up with their demands feeds the myth that they made history. But a myth is what it is.' The headmistress paused and looked around the class, daring anyone to disagree. When no one did she continued, 'In this country we proceed by argument. Reasonable, peaceful argument. But activists aren't interested in argument. They never have been.' Then – 'Edith!' she said sharply. 'Explain your frown.'

'Activists?' said Edie.

'Oh yes. Make no mistake, the suffragettes were activists.' Miss Fotheringay pronounced the word with distaste. 'They achieved nothing then, just as activists seldom achieve anything now. Their cause may be right, but their methods are potty.'

'What—' Janet began, then stopped herself.

'Janet?' Miss Fotheringay said, smiling. 'I sense you disagree. Well? Do we have an activist in our midst? We all know you're a rebel. Perhaps finally you have found yourself a cause?'

Miss Fotheringay watched her expectantly, but Janet glowered. The rest of the class giggled nervously, but Edie was baffled. She sensed that Fothy was taunting Janet with something. But what?

'Deeds not words,' Miss Fotheringay said briskly, pointing back to the board. 'I'm glad you brought it up, Janet, because that is the subject of your lunch-time essay.'

'No way!' said Janet, looking around at the rest of the class in consternation. 'Why me?'

'Because it will interest you,' Miss Fotheringay said. 'And it will keep you out of trouble.'

'Why did Fothy say that, about keeping Janet out of trouble?' asked Anastasia, as she and Edie walked away from the dining room arm in arm. 'It's as though she knew we were going to corner her.'

'It's just her way of talking,' said Edie quickly. But Miss Fotheringay's apparent prescience on the matter made her uneasy too. 'Let's wait a bit,' she said.

But Anastasia was determined and insisted that she and Edie hover outside the lower school prep room, where Janet had been sent to write her essay under the supervision of Mr Robinson. 'Then we can pounce on her as soon as she comes out.'

If Janet was feeling chastened by her confrontation with Miss Fotheringay she did not let it show. When the bell for afternoon lessons rang, she sauntered into the corridor with her usual lop-sided gait.

'Hello, you two. You look . . . conspiratorial. What's the plan?'

Typical Janet, thought Edie. *Never, what's the problem? Always, what's the plan?*

'We want to talk to you,' said Anastasia.

'Talk away.'

'Not here. We need to go somewhere private,' said Edie.

'Sounds really scary,' said Janet, grinning. 'Would you like to handcuff me? I feel as though I'm under arrest.'

'You are,' said Anastasia, seizing one of Janet's arms, and motioning Edie to take the other. 'And you're coming to my dormitory.'

'Wait a minute,' said Janet, shaking free. 'I was only joking.'

'Yes,' said Anastasia. 'But we're not. We need you to answer some questions.'

'And if I refuse?' asked Janet. She was walking alongside them now, her tone casual.

'If you refuse,' Anastasia said meaningfully, 'we will have to assume the worst.'

'Well, I know that is the Stolonov way. What did Edie have to do by the way to get back into favour?' she asked mockingly. 'Did money change hands?'

Anastasia looked furious and Edie put a hand on her arm to calm her. 'I didn't have to do anything,' she said quietly to Janet. 'Anastasia just worked something out.'

'And now we've worked out something else,' Anastasia said. They had reached the door of Charlbury. Anastasia held it open, and stared at Janet in silence as she walked inside. When they were all in the dormitory Anastasia slammed the door behind them, and faced Janet with her hands on her hips.

'Well?' Janet said, smiling.

'The person who released my ferrets that night was wearing Edie's dressing gown,' Anastasia said, looking at Janet with an expression of cold triumph.

Janet frowned. Edie watched her face closely, searching for any sign of guilt. But Newgirl's expression gave nothing away.

'We know that because it had mud on it – Alice saw Matron take it away to be washed the next morning,' Edie said carefully, unnerved by Janet's silence.

'And when we did fire drill, you wore Edie's dressing gown,' Anastasia added in a rush. 'That's when we realized it must have been you who wore it that night. It's much too long for Edie, she always trips over in it, but you—'

Edie winced. Somehow the proof didn't sound as foolproof as it should.

'Ah, I see,' said Janet. 'The dressing gown clue. How completely thrilling. Two missing ferrets and a muddied red robe. Well, well, Inspector Clouseau's nothing on you two.'

'Oh, shut up, Janet!' Edie spat. 'Just tell us straight: did you or did you not release Anastasia's ferrets? Simple question, simple answer. Yes or no?'

'We know—' began Anastasia.

'Shh,' said Edie, taking charge. 'Let her answer.'

Janet's face was completely calm. 'No,' she said, looking at each of her accusers in turn. 'No, I did not release Anastasia's ferrets.' Her voice was so firm that for a moment even Anastasia seemed lost for words.

'And what about—' Anastasia began, before Edie silenced her with a meaningful look. If they accosted Janet about the key, she would know Edie had been prying in her post.

'What about?' Janet asked sarcastically.

'Nothing,' Edie said.

'Well then, if you don't mind,' Janet said, brushing past them, 'there is somewhere I have to be. Schoolgirl sleuthing is all very well, but some of us have bigger fish to fry. Oops. Sorry, Edie. I didn't mean to remind you of *your* pet trauma.'

'God, she's horrible,' said Anastasia, watching Janet go. 'Oh, Edie, how could you ever have thought you liked her?'

A Penny Drops

On Saturday morning came the news that Anastasia's gating had been repealed for good behaviour. She and Edie at once cooked up a plan to go into the village together for what would be their first legitimate outing that term.

'Have you seen Janet since lunch?' Anastasia asked, as she and Edie signed their names out in the book.

'No. Why?'

'I just don't want her spoiling our fun.'

'She won't,' said Edie, sounding more bullish than she felt. Something about Janet's denial continued to bother her. It wasn't that she thought she was innocent. Quite the opposite. But why had she been so emphatic? *'No, I did not release Anastasia's ferrets,'* she had said, in a tone of such conviction.

Why hadn't she just confessed? Janet wasn't usually afraid of getting into trouble.

'I'm so glad we're agreed about her at last,' Anastasia said in a happy voice. 'She's such a cheat! But let's not think about her now. I want a whole blessed afternoon not mentioning the J-word at all.'

Edie smiled. There was something infectious about Anastasia's mood.

'Oh, Edie, it feels just like old times,' Anastasia said, swinging her purse in the air. 'I haven't been out for so long, I've got enough pocket money for tea at the Ritz. Isn't it a pity the Ritz isn't closer? I haven't been there for weeks!' She prattled on excitedly, skipping through the puddles, clearly thrilled to be released. It had been raining heavily all week, but this afternoon the clouds had cleared as if to honour the occasion. 'Two whole hours of freedom! We'll eat every bun in the Blue Kettle! We'll set the church bells ringing! We'll paint the village pink!'

'Red,' Edie corrected her, but Anastasia was in full flow.

'Out! Damned spot!' she cried, after pressing a berry between her fingers and staining her skin with juice. 'Oh, Edie, isn't *Macbeth* the best play ever?'

Anastasia was in such high spirits, that when Miss Mannering passed them in her car Edie feared she might flag her down for a lift.

'Poor old Man!' Anastasia sighed, waving boisterously as the car went past. 'A lonesome spinster born into a life of toil!'

'Blimey! You are in a poetic mood,' Edie said.

'Hard not to be when you've spent a weekend reading *Macbeth* with Fothy,' Anastasia giggled.

'Oh,' Edie said, thinking about the copy of *Macbeth* Fothy had given her at the beginning of term, and feeling oddly left out by this revelation. 'But you said she was worrying about her father all the time and that you hardly saw her.'

'That's true. But on Saturday evening she suddenly relaxed and we did some scenes together. Then the phone rang and she disappeared again, but – oh, Edie! I can see why you like staying with her so much. She's such fun when she's not being a headmistress and when you've got her all to yourself. And you should have heard her Lady Macbeth! *Come, you spirits / That tend on mortal thoughts, unsex me here, / And fill me from the crown to the toe topful / Of direst cruelty!*' Anastasia flung her arms, clutching at her forehead with a dramatic sigh. 'Aaaaah!'

'Idiot,' Edie murmured affectionately.

But Anastasia suddenly pulled herself upright, and stood staring at something, startled: 'Hey, Edie, look! Look over there!' she whispered, pointing through a gap in the hedge beside the lane.

Edie leant down to see, and gave a low whistle. It was Janet, making her own way to the village, cutting down cross-country across the fields.

Edie wasn't surprised to see her out alone. But she was struck by the purposeful way Janet was hurrying down the hill, as if she was late for something – or feared she was being followed. Edie wondered how she intended to amuse herself. She imagined her going on her own into the village shop, stocking up on more cans of lemonade to hide in her bedside table, and ordering hot chocolate for one at the Blue Kettle, and felt a muddled rush of pity.

'Perhaps I should call her,' she said uncertainly.

'Oh, don't!' Anastasia said, pulling her back from the hedge. 'Please, Edie, we agreed. Why can't you just hate her, like I do?'

'I don't know,' said Edie. This was the truth. She had every reason to hate Janet – both for how she had behaved at Folly and for the way she had let Edie take the blame for the ferrets. But she couldn't forget how Janet had ruffled her hair and said '*Wilson's my friend, aren't you?*' Or the sadness she had seen on her face when she had thought no one was looking. And Edie was still puzzling over the exchange between Fothy and Janet in class – as if there were something both of them were hiding.

When they arrived in the village Anastasia wanted to go straight for tea in the Blue Kettle. 'Before the fifth form come and hog all the tables,' she explained, tugging Edie through the door, into a misted interior of milky fumes and checked tablecloths. The tearoom was already almost full. Members of the lower school rarely came to the Blue Kettle without their parents – their pocket money didn't stretch to it – but two groups of senior girls had bagged the tables in the window, and Matron was sitting tucked in the corner with one of the school cooks, next to a glass counter stacked with spiced buns and doughnuts, and elaborately-iced cakes. Edie and Anastasia made their choices, and settled at a draughty table near the door.

'If Janet comes in here don't ask her to join us,' Anastasia said, pointedly removing the extra chair from their table.

'Oh, come on,' Edie said, smiling mischievously. 'Let's lure her in and stuff her with cream cakes, then when she's about to pop we'll tie her to her chair and force her into confessing!'

'Stop it!' Anastasia said, shuddering. 'This is not a joking matter, Edie. I don't want her anywhere near us, not today. I can't look at her without thinking what she did to my darling Precious and Treasure! Oh, Edie, you can't imagine how much I miss them! Sometimes I wake up at night wondering where they are . . .' Anastasia's voice trailed off in a plaintive tone. 'Do you think they're missing me?' she asked feebly.

'Probably not,' said Edie, hoping to steer the conversation away from maudlin waters.

'But what do you think they're doing?' said Anastasia, insistent.

'I expect they're having a good time, like us. Painting the town pink,' Edie said.

Anastasia looked cheered by this idea. 'I'm glad I've got *you* back, Edie,' she said, running her finger down the menu with relish.

But Edie couldn't concentrate on the day's choice of

buns. 'Look, I know we agreed we wouldn't talk about Janet,' she said, 'but I just don't like mysteries.'

'You sound like Fothy speaking on the phone to the Man,' Anastasia laughed. 'Did you know by the way that the Man's name is Diana? Can you think of anything more unlikely?' She ran her finger down the laminated menu card, her brief prick of tears over the ferrets swallowed by an impish smile. *How changeable she is,* Edie thought, not for the first time.

'What was she saying on the phone? Was she talking about Janet?' she asked, curious.

'You bet she was,' Anastasia said, with a toss of the head. 'It was Janet this, and Janet that. I suppose you can't accuse her of not caring. A weekend off from school, and all they seem to do is talk about us.'

'But what were they saying? Janet this and Janet that what?'

'Well, lacking your supersonic ears I only heard one half of the conversation. And that was Fothy's solemn voice saying, "It's better that they don't see each other. Trouble is bound to ensue." What does ensue mean?'

'Follow,' said Edie impatiently.

'That's what I thought. Well, I suppose she was right about that.'

'But who did she mean by "they"? Please, Anastasia, try and remember. We're meant to be investigating her – remember?'

'She meant you, of course,' Anastasia shrugged. 'At least, that's how I took it. You know Janet kept getting you into trouble, so that's why Fothy said you shouldn't see each other. Sorry, Edie, I'd thought I'd told you. Anyway, you can hardly be surprised.'

'But she said this while I was spending the weekend with Janet! I told her I was taking her home with me. If she wanted to keep us apart why didn't she try and stop it? It doesn't make sense.'

'Oh, Edie, please stop trying to de-strange everything. It's so exhausting. Fothy just thinks Janet's bad for you. And it so happens I think the same. Oh God, Edie, what's wrong with us? We promised not to mention the J-word and here we are talking about nothing else.'

Anastasia was clearly sick of the subject, but Edie was puzzled. Who was it that Miss Fotheringay wanted to keep Janet away from? And why was Janet so determined always to go to the village without a walking partner? If there was someone she was meeting secretly, then her furtive behaviour would make sense.

'Oh, Edie, I'm so glad we're best friends again,' Anastasia said suddenly, clasping her hand. 'Just imagine it, Edie – if – if *Newgirl* had managed to break us up!'

'She wouldn't have,' Edie said, her thoughts moving back to the solitary figure cutting across the field with an air of secret intent.

'Edie?' Anastasia asked querulously. 'Oh, what is it, Edie! Why are you always thinking about her! Can't we just pretend she doesn't exist, just for one afternoon?' Then – 'All right, a deal!' she announced. 'I'll stop going on about the ferrets if you stop going on about her. How fair is that?'

But before any bargain could be struck, Janet

appeared at the teashop door. She stood there for a moment, peering inside, but when she saw Edie and Anastasia she turned and hurried away.

'Good riddance,' Anastasia muttered, but Edie was intrigued. Who had Janet been looking for?

She thought better than to share her preoccupations with Anastasia, and she did not mention Janet again as they finished tea, and wandered down to the village shop. But as they were emerging with their supplies, Anastasia grabbed Edie's arm:

'I don't believe it!' she whispered, gesturing across the road – and Edie looked up in time to see Janet slipping through the door of the pub.

Edie stared after her. Janet might *look* a lot older than them, but she was still only thirteen, far too young to go into a pub. But she had been to the village on her own before, and not wanted anyone to go with her. Was this the reason: because she had a secret meeting with someone in the Drunken Drunk?

'You stay here, I'm going to follow her,' Edie said quietly, handing Anastasia her bag. 'Just trust me, Ansti,' she pleaded. 'I'll explain everything later.'

'Don't be an idiot, Edie, you can't go into the pub. If anyone sees you you'll be done for. If Janet wants to get herself expelled, then let her—'

'Janet's up to something, and I've got to find out who she's seeing, that's all,' Edie said, her eyes fixed on the pub door.

Anastasia looked at her, as if weighing something up. Then, 'All right,' she ceded. 'But I'm coming too.'

'But—'

'Just trust me, Edie,' Anastasia teased, taking her arm and steering her across the lane. 'Walk straight in, then you can see who she's with since you're so determined to find out, then we can walk straight out again. And if anyone asks, say we're just wanting to use the loo.

'If you're caught—' Edie began.

But Anastasia had already led them inside.

The lighting in the pub was low, with the daylight dimmed by the net curtains hanging at the two tiny windows set deep into the wall. There were two men sitting with pints of beer at the bar, and a few people scattered about the tables, but no sign of Janet.

'You here for the protest meeting?' the barman asked, looking up over the pint of beer he was pulling from a brass tap.

Edie looked blank. 'Private room to the left,' he said, nodding in that direction.

'Thanks,' Edie murmured, making towards it.

But just then the door to the room opened, and a group of people streamed into the bar.

As they entered Edie recognized two of the boys with rainbow-coloured hair from the horse fair who had been petitioning against the building of the road through the woods around the tower.

Edie looked at them curiously, and realized that the protest meeting which the publican had referred to must be about Mesmere Wood. Since the horse fair, the campaign seemed to have gathered force. At the fair, there had been five of them handing out leaflets to whoever walked past, but now Edie watched as twenty or thirty people, some old, some young, crowded around two long tables by the bar.

Seeing the girls standing there, one came over and gave them a leaflet.

'Thank you,' Edie said shyly. 'How's it . . . I mean, do you think you're going to be able to stop the bulldozers?'

Edie wondered if the protesters knew who was behind the building project – and what they would think if they discovered that the prince's own daughter was attending their meeting.

The man smiled. 'We wouldn't be protesting if we thought we couldn't. We've got quite a presence there now. The police will have a job clearing the tents.'

'Tents?' Edie asked stupidly.

The man looked surprised. 'Haven't you seen the camp? We've set them up all around the tower – we've been there four weeks now.'

Edie frowned. She could understand now why Miss Fotheringay had been so strict about the woods being out of bounds. But then she gave a start: there was Janet, looking alert and excited as she appeared, clutching a stash of papers, and squeezed next to a man on the end of a bench.

'What's she doing here?' Anastasia whispered, tugging Edie back towards the door.

'Protesting, I suppose,' Edie said slowly. 'Like everyone else.'

Anastasia looked confused. 'But – but if everyone's protesting about my father's tower, then why didn't we know?'

'Because we have been living in our sheltered little schoolgirl world, where even the goings-on in our own village are a mystery to us,' Edie replied. 'Janet, on the other hand . . .' She thought of Janet's solitary disappearances from school and felt a start of admiration. Edie was in no doubt now where the missing sausages had gone. She wondered if more had gone since.

But when she looked back across the room a moment later, Janet had gone.

'Where is she?' Edie whispered.

'Over there,' Anastasia said, nodding towards a door at the other end of the bar. Edie and Anastasia followed, and found themselves in a small corridor, with voices audible through a door which had been left ajar.

'Hello, Angel,' came Janet's voice. 'Cool to see you. That was a good meeting, wasn't it?'

'Hi there, Josie. Yeah. The action's hotting up. You on a bunk?'

'No, we get allowed out on two-hour release on Saturdays,' Janet replied.

'OK, that's cool. See you later, then. Remember, what's the word?'

'Dunsinane,' Janet replied.

'Good girl. You might need it. Informers are everywhere.'

There followed a short silence, during which Edie's mind spun: 'The ferrets, Anastasia,' she whispered excitedly, 'do you remember, they weren't given to you at all . . . they were for someone called Josie.'

'And we thought there wasn't a Josie at Knight's Haddon,' Anastasia said, nodding grimly.

Edie frowned, as things tumbled into place. 'Do you remember, Anastasia, the way Janet said, "No. I did not release Anastasia's ferrets." She *did* release them – but they weren't yours. That's why she was able to deny it so convincingly. Because so far as she was concerned, she wasn't lying! She released *her* ferrets, not yours!'

'Some excuse!' Anastasia said darkly. Then, 'Shh!' she said, as the door suddenly swung open.

Janet sauntered out.

'Janet!' Edie said, feeling caught out.

'You!' said Janet, glaring. 'What are you doing here?'

'We followed you,' said Anastasia.

'Listen. If it's about the ferrets—'

'It's not,' said Edie.

'Yes it is!' said Anastasia.

'Oh, buzz off,' said Janet. 'I'm not interested in your trifling detective work. There's something going on here which actually matters.' She glanced over her shoulder, hesitant, and when she spoke her voice came in an excited rush: 'This lot are going to stop the woods being cut down. Tomorrow. But they need more people. There were others, there were more, but some of them have gone now, back up north . . . they didn't know the police were coming, otherwise they wouldn't have left, and now we're short. Come with me, why don't you?' This last was addressed to Edie in a breathless, urgent voice.

Edie had never seen Janet so lit up.

'Come away, Edie,' Anastasia said, tugging at her arm. 'She wants to get expelled, remember, but we don't.'

Edie frowned, suddenly wishing Anastasia would be quiet. Janet clearly had no idea that Prince Stolonov was behind the development, else she would surely have said.

'Oh, come *on*, Edie,' Anastasia said, tugging her arm.

But Janet looked at Edie hard, as if Anastasia wasn't there. 'Don't you want to help? Don't you want to be part of something larger than your stupid little world at Knight's Haddon?'

Edie just stared. She had a sudden image of bulldozers crashing into the woods, and of Janet rising from the undergrowth to repel them, her red dressing gown shining in the moonlight . . .

'Don't be stupid, Edie!' Anastasia pleaded. 'Don't get involved!'

Edie looked at her urgently. 'But, Ansti, *you* don't want this development to go ahead. You more than anyone,' she added, lowering her voice. 'Why don't you want to join the protest?'

'Because it won't stop it happening. It's like Fothy said in the suffragette lesson. And Janet doesn't care about the woods. You know what her game is. She just wants to get sent home – and what she'd like more than anything else is to bring you down with her.'

'Game, eh?' said Janet.

'Please, Janet, wait,' Edie protested. 'Please explain—'

'No time,' said Janet. 'I need to catch Angel.' And then she slipped away, pushing open the door at the end of the corridor which gave on to the lane.

'We'd better get out of here too,' said Anastasia making to follow her. 'We can't stay in a *pub*, Edie.'

'Wait, first I want to find out what's going on,' said Edie, pulling her back into the bar. 'I want to know when the bulldozers are going in.'

But when they moved back into the main bar, the room was almost deserted. Edie looked around her, baffled. The group had disappeared as quickly as it had come.

'What were you thinking of, Edie?' Anastasia asked her crossly. 'Anyone would think you wanted to join them!'

'Maybe I do,' Edie replied, feeling increasingly irritated by Anastasia's presence.

'Don't you dare!' Anastasia said furiously. 'I'm telling you, Edie, don't!'

Edie turned back to the bar, thinking she would enquire where the group had gone. But when she approached it she was aware of the barman looking at her suspiciously, and lost her nerve.

Then, swallowing, she thought of Babka and her grandmother's favourite tipple. 'Two cherry brandies, please,' she said.

The barman looked surprised. And then his glance slid along the counter. Edie, following it, was horrified to feel it rest on a small stout figure, dressed to kill in a scarf of many stripes.

'M-miss Mannering,' Edie faltered.

'Cancel that order if you would, Andrew,' said the deputy headmistress of Knight's Haddon. 'Unless you want to go to prison.'

19

KNIGHT'S HADDON

Telling Tales and Owning Up

'This is my trouble, Anastasia,' Edie whispered as the Man marched them outside. 'Stay out of it, promise? And let me do the talking.'

'But—'

Edie pinched her, hard. 'No buts, just promise. Remember, you owe me. I'm in charge of this story, not you. You mustn't tell anyone – not about Janet being Josie. Not about the ferrets, not about the protest, not about her going into the pub. Say you promise?'

Anastasia squirmed but she knew she had no choice. 'Promise,' she murmured under her breath.

This was all they had time for before the Man ushered them into the back of the car. The deputy said nothing to break the silence and nor did they.

When they arrived at Knight's Haddon she did not park in her usual place in the school forecourt, which was milling with people, but drove instead to the back of the West Tower where they couldn't be seen. Once there, she switched off the engine and locked the doors.

'Well,' she said, looking from one to the other of her charges in the car mirror as the windscreen wipers continued to battle the rain that was now falling heavily. 'What have you got to say for yourselves?'

'We're really sorry,' said Anastasia. 'We were just—'

'No, we weren't,' Edie cut in roughly. '*We* weren't doing anything. It was only me, Miss Mannering. Anastasia tried to persuade me not to.'

'Not to . . . what?'

'Go into the pub. She begged me not to and then she followed me in.'

'The point—' Anastasia broke in, frowning.

'That is the point,' Edie said, enforcing her message with a kick.

'I see. And what possessed you, Edith Wilson, to go into the Drunken Duck? You are surely not unaware that it is out of bounds even to members of the Upper Sixth, let alone mere—?' Miss Mannering eyed Edie disdainfully in the mirror, as if challenging her to find the right word.

But Edie said nothing.

'She did it for a dare,' Anastasia threw in a little too keenly – as if the idea had just struck her.

'Indeed? And who issued you with such an interesting challenge?'

Edie stayed mum.

'Really, girls, I haven't got time for this. Would one of you kindly tell me exactly what is going on.'

'Anastasia can't tell you,' said Edie, 'because she doesn't know.'

'Very well. I can see that your persuasively ill-rehearsed double act is holding us up. Anastasia, you will see me in my office first thing tomorrow morning. Edith, you will come with me now.'

Edie followed Miss Mannering into the school, casting furtive glances to her right and left. She wondered where Fothy was, remembering how the headmistress had ridden to Edie's rescue on her very first night ever at the school, when the Man had caught her sneaking about after lights out. Edie had thought then that the Man was going to eat her, but Fothy had swooped down the corridor like a beautiful sorceress, and somehow magicked all the trouble away.

But Fothy wouldn't make things better now, Edie thought, biting her lip to stop the tears which suddenly threatened. Even if the headmistress did rescue her from the Man, it would only be in order to take her back to the West Tower, and grill her and grill her, goading, cajoling, probing, until finally Edie would be able to take no more. Then she would break down and tell the headmistress that it was Janet they had followed into the pub, and everyone in the school would know that it was Edith Wilson who had sneaked. And only Anastasia would understand how hard she had tried not to tell, and how impossible it was when Fothy took you into her study, and talked about your mother, and went on and on and on about *in loco parentis* and looked at you with her searchlight eyes.

'Edith Wilson. I am not the fool you seem to take me for.' The Man's eyes glared.

'I didn't say that!'

'No. But then you haven't said anything much, except, "Yes. No. Don't know." It's been a peculiarly unrewarding exchange, from my point of view.'

'I'm sorry.'

'Cherry brandies in the Drunken Duck? What can you have been thinking of?'

I wasn't thinking, I was following, Edie wanted to cry out. *And so would you have been, if you'd seen what I'd seen.*

'You do realize the gravity of your offence? The case calls for immediate suspension for the rest of the term with a Final Warning attached.'

'Yes,' Edie said. She was terrified at the prospect of being sent home for the rest of the term. And what if the Final Warning meant she could *never* come back? But the interview had taken on a remote quality, as if part of a baffling dream. She found her eyes roving around the Man's office, noting vaguely how different it was to Miss Fotheringay's. The walls were bare, except for a series of metal bookshelves which looked as though they would not be out of place in a torture chamber. They were filled with black box files, and hung with paper sheets, showing schedules of work written out. There was nothing in the office that could be described as personal except for a dusty shelf of school trophies – mainly for chess.

Respect, thought Edie. She had a sudden memory of Babka blindly moving the figures around her faded chessboard, bad-tempered even in victory as she made her granddaughter play her against the clock. Edie would never have known the Man for a chess player too.

'You have a particular fondness for cherry brandy?'

'No-o,' said Edie, surprised out of her reverie and into the truth. 'But I was thirsty.'

'You were thirsty and so you ordered a drink you don't like?'

'I don't think I like any alcohol,' Edie replied simply.

'So in that case, why didn't you ask for a glass of water, or an orange juice?'

Edie looked puzzled. Then her face cleared. 'I thought you had to order alcohol in – somewhere like that.'

This is a child who has never been bought a soft drink in a pub, Miss Mannering noted to herself. When she next spoke her voice was kinder than before.

'I was watching you for several minutes, before accosting you. Oh yes,' she went on, noting Edie's surprise. 'Teachers can be devious too, in a good cause. And I observed that you and Anastasia appeared to be having some sort of an altercation. Would you care to tell me what it was about?'

But Edie knew she could explain nothing without explaining everything. And that would mean telling the Man about Janet, and her links with the protesters at

Mesmere Wood. And nothing would make Edie sneak. Instead, she seized her chance to get Anastasia out of trouble.

'Yes,' she said, 'the altercation was because I wanted to go into the pub, and Anastasia didn't.'

The Man sighed. 'I am loath to disturb Miss Fotheringay with this matter. Her father, as I think you know, is very ill and she has gone to be with him this weekend.'

'I-I didn't know that,' Edie said.

Miss Mannering looked at her closely. 'I have some-times worried this term that you have presumed on Miss Fotheringay's special fondness for you, Edith,' she said at length. 'It is an unusual situation. Her friendship with your mother . . .'

Edie felt hot with the injustice of this accusation. She wasn't in trouble because she presumed on Fothy's 'special fondness'. She was in trouble because she refused to. And as for bringing her mother into it . . . it was enough to make Edie scream with rage.

But still she kept her peace. And Miss Mannering, at the end of her tether, interpreted her silence as sullen-ness.

'I see I have touched a nerve,' she said coldly, as she picked up the telephone.

Rumours of Edie's likely suspension flew around the school. Anastasia found herself outside the open door of the lower school common room, and couldn't help but listen in to Phoebe and a group of first years.

'Is it because she let the ferrets out?'

'Should think so.'

'We knew she was lying! Do you remember, Clare, when the Prent found her in the animal house?'

'I knew she was lying about something, but I never thought she was guilty. I still don't.'

'Ha, ha, Clare Fairweather's got a crush on Edie Wilson!'

'I do not!'

'She's definitely guilty,' said Phoebe. 'The rest of us knew it weeks ago!'

'So now Fothy believes it too?'

'No, no, it's not Fothy who's suspended her. Fothy's away.'

'Who then?'

'The Man, of course.'

'That makes sense!'

'But the Man won't actually send her away until Fothy comes back.'

'And when Fothy comes back she'll probably rescind the suspension.'

'My mother says teachers shouldn't have favourites.'

'Hah! Tell that to the head of Knight's Haddon!'

'What I don't get is why Anastasia made up with her.'

'She'll be regretting it now.'

That's my cue, thought Anastasia, walking into the common room with a toss of her hair.

There was an embarrassed silence as Anastasia looked at the first years accusingly, one by one. *'Je ne regrette rien. De rien,'* she said in her soft, sweet voice, before turning on her heel and going to the lockers under the window. She knelt down in front of hers, and made a show of burying her head in its jumble of contents.

'Come again?'

'She means she doesn't regret anything,' explained Phoebe. 'But then she would say that, wouldn't she?'

'Why would she?'

'Because people like her don't like being wrong.'

'*C'est de toi qui tu parles,*' Anastasia called out, slamming shut her locker, and giving up all pretence of not listening.

'Eh?'

Phoebe was now strangely reluctant to provide a translation.

'I mean,' said Anastasia, standing up, 'that Phoebe is speaking about herself. She doesn't like being wrong. But she is, in fact, barking up completely the wrong branch.'

'Oh yes?' said Phoebe, blushing an ugly red. 'So what's Edie been suspended for then?'

Anastasia glared at her, moving her lips as though rehearsing a speech she wasn't sure whether or not she should make. 'We were caught, as it happens,' she said, 'by the Man, as we were having a drink in the Drunken Duck.'

This was news – and even Phoebe could not hide her startled admiration.

'So why haven't you been suspended as well?' asked Clare.

Anastasia bit her lip. She knew she couldn't break her

promise to Edie about not telling. Not after everything else she had done wrong that term! But *why* had Edie been so insistent? Janet had let her take the blame for something she hadn't done – so surely that was reason enough to tell on her now? But Edie would never play sneak. Anastasia supposed it was something to do with the way Fothy tried to prise bits of information out of her. Edie always had to prove that she wasn't the person other people accused her of being – the person who even her best friend had accused her of being. Anastasia felt sick with remorse when she thought of this. Edie had been so forgiving, but she didn't deserve it! Of course she mustn't break her word.

'Quite right,' sneered Phoebe, breaking into Anastasia's reverie. 'Makes no sense. Why haven't you been suspended as well?'

'Perhaps I will be,' she said. 'Or perhaps Edie won't be,' she added, looking at the door, 'when the reason for our presence in the Drunken Duck owns up.'

The others followed Anastasia's withering gaze to see Newgirl standing in the doorway. She looked even more dishevelled than usual, with her shirt hanging from her tunic and her socks slumped around her ankles.

'There's telling tales, there's owning up and there's minding your own business,' said Janet coolly. 'And I know which camp I'm in.'

Edie was told that she would be collected in the morning by her Aunt Sophia.

'It is sometimes easier to write an explanation than to

speak it,' said the Man, leaving her in the san for the night equipped with a bowl of thin tomato soup, two slices of unbuttered toast, and a pen and paper. 'Let's see what you come up with.'

Edie stared at the piece of paper the Man had left.

A written confession, she thought, looking down in despair to see that the Man had written the first seven words for her.

I went to the Drunken Duck because . . .

I saw another girl go there and I have reason to believe the other girl has a secret life and I am afraid for her, Edie continued, then stopped, biting her lip. Was she afraid for Janet – or *of* Janet?

I don't want to tell on the other girl because . . . Edie bit her lip until it bled.

Then a mood of something like recklessness seized her. She was in as much trouble as it was possible to be, but she had at least one thing to hold on to: she hadn't sneaked. She could be proud of that, whatever happened next. She smiled, grimly, and picked up her pen.

I went to the Drunken Duck because I felt like it. Then I felt ill and ordered a cherry brandy. I ordered one for me and one for luck. End of story, jackanory.

Grey Area

'You're a fool.'

'I'm not listening to you! I shouldn't even be in this car! The Man thought Aunt Sophia was coming.'

'As I understand it, the Man – as you so amusingly describe your deputy headmistress – could not get rid of you fast enough.'

'It's nothing to do with you!'

'Of course it's to do with me. I'm your guardian.'

'No you're not! You just pretended to be when it suited you!'

Cousin Charles said nothing and Edie immediately wished her words unspoken. The question of her guardianship was a grey area. When her grandmother had gone blind, she had been sent to live with Aunt Sophia, who had seemed only too pleased when their rich cousin Charles had unexpectedly swooped in and offered to send Edie away to school. And then there was Miss Fotheringay, who sometimes behaved as if Edie belonged to her. But as to the legalities, no one ever discussed them.

Cousin Charles shuffled in his seat, with an air of irritation. 'I thought you were happy at school,' he said after a pause.

'What's that got to do with anything?'

'It might have induced you not to rock the boat by buying Anastasia cherry brandies in the pub! Good God!' Cousin Charles snorted. 'Even I didn't start drinking until I was fourteen!'

'I didn't want her to come with me! It's not my fault that she followed me.'

'No doubt she followed you for the reason you say. For God's sake, Edith, remember your place. It's not Anastasia's job to keep you out of trouble. The other way round, remember?'

Edie bit her lip. Why did Charles still have to talk as though she was Anastasia's servant? It was true that she had first been sent to Knight's Haddon to look after Anastasia – but that was more than a year ago. Things were different now.

'Who said anything about having a job? Anastasia's my best friend,' she said sullenly. 'Of course we care what happens to each other. Maybe you find that hard to understand. Maybe all your friends are also jobs.'

Charles threw her an amused look. 'Maybe they are,' he said. Then, with practised cruelty, 'And maybe yours are too. More than you think anyway.'

'What are you talking about?'

'Work it out.'

Charles's words were like the faint hum of thunder before the storm, and Edie had a sudden sense of the world darkening around her.

'Has it not occurred to you, Edith, that it is Prince Stolonov who generously pays your school fees?'

Edie looked at him, stunned. It had never occurred to her that the prince was her benefactor. She had always thought she attended Knight's Haddon on a bursary. Miss Fotheringay had said as much when Edie had been ill last year, after the kidnap: '*We have bursaries, Edith. If you want to stay, I'm sure I could fix it.*' Edie remembered her words exactly.

'Come on, Edie, stop looking so tragic. I expect you've got a bit of credit in the Stolonov bank. He's not going to pull the rug just like that. Though wasn't there some trouble with a horse fair earlier this term? Oh dear, you really haven't been concentrating.'

'That wasn't my fault!' Edie said, recoiling. It was all disgusting, everything he said, everything he implied.

Phoebe's words about Anastasia came ringing back: '*It was only a matter of time before she gave Edie her job back.*'

Did everyone else know the humiliating truth of her position? Or had Anastasia been sworn to secrecy by her father? Edie could imagine them plotting together on the deck of the prince's yacht, and felt something twist inside. How could she and Anastasia be true best friends if Edie was in her family's pay?

'You must have known you were some sort of charity case,' said Cousin Charles, sounding impatient.

But Edie hadn't known. And by failing to work it out, she had walked blindly into Cousin Charles's taunt. And Miss Fotheringay had misled her too. Why hadn't she admitted that it was the prince who paid her fees? Edie remembered how Miss Fotheringay had dodged the question when Edie had asked her who had bought the tower, and the dismissive tone with which she had swept aside any talk of objection: *The tower is private property . . . any protest will be an exercise in futility . . .* She felt a rush of resentment. Was everyone in the prince's pay?

'Well, are you going to join me for lunch? Brace up, Edie, for heaven's sake.'

Edie looked up and around to find that they had come to a purring stop outside the Drunken Duck. 'I can't go in there,' she said, squirming to recall her hurried exit the previous afternoon.

Cousin Charles smiled. 'I thought this was a regular haunt. Come on, it's got a dining room. Infants allowed.'

'I'm not hungry.'

'You will be. God alone knows what the food situation is at St Benedict's.'

'St Benedict's?' Edie asked. St Benedict's was the nursing home where her Polish grandmother lived. 'Are we going to visit Babka?'

'A long visit, in your case,' Charles replied. 'They're putting you up. Your Aunt Sophia pretends she is up to her elbows in something disgusting to do with farming, and I can't have you in London – too much on – so Babka it is.'

This was not what Edie had been expecting. 'But – but I can't stay at a nursing home.'

'Yes, you can. I've fixed it. And make the most of it, old girl. The room's not cheap.'

'But – I – everyone there's old!'

'Don't look so glum,' said Cousin Charles. 'It might be fun. They probably all drink cherry brandy!'

Edie felt Charles's eyes assessing her reaction to the news and determined not to show her dismay.

'Fine. But I don't want any lunch. At least not from here,' she said.

'And I don't want any from anywhere else. Here, you can buy yourself a sandwich then and eat it on the bench outside.' He looked up at the sky. 'There's always the bus-shelter if it starts raining again.'

Edie took the proffered five-pound note with a scowl.

'Charming,' murmured her cousin as he disappeared inside.

Charles Rodriguez sat down in the restaurant of the Drunken Duck and examined the menu with a curl of his lip. The list of familiar dishes filled him with gloom. Why was it so difficult to get a decent meal in the English countryside? Surely the through traffic of Knight's Haddon parents would support one of those new-fangled gastro-pubs?

Then again, perhaps not, he thought ruefully, remembering the strictness of the access arrangements. 'The whole point about that ghastly school is that you only see the children twice a term at most,' his cousin Sophia had said when she had rung him about Edie's latest escapade. 'And the whole point about Edie is that she prefers it at that prison anyway. I can't think what's gone wrong.'

Charles couldn't think either, and he had a feeling that Edie wasn't going to tell him.

'She's more likely to open up to you than to me,' Sophia had said. 'She was closer than a clam last time she came here. She brought a friend, who knew exactly how to have a relaxed holiday time. The contrast was grim.'

Charles had a pretty shrewd idea of what passed for relaxed holiday times at Folly Farm and why Edie hated them. And he knew too how much more guarded Edie appeared when you met her in the company of another girl her age. He had once taken her out to tea with his goddaughter Anastasia, and Edie had sat mute and accusing while Anastasia prattled away. But he also knew that there was another side to Edie – he had seen how alert and interested she was in the company of Prince Stolonov, Anastasia's father, with whom she was a great favourite.

Not any more, he thought now as he imagined the prince's likely reaction to news that Edie had lured Anastasia into a village pub! He was conscious of having been cruel to Edie, telling her about the fees arrangement, but really the child had to know some time.

Aaaagh! What a bore it was to be involved at all! Charles had no interest in children. Anastasia was different, she was enchanting, she made an effort, and she would one day inherit the art collection which Charles had built for her father. But as for Edie, it was bad enough to be saddled with transporting the wretched girl from school to the stinking nursing home. He was damned if he was going to spend any more time thinking about her too!

He ordered his lunch and retrieved his smart phone from his pocket, to discover to his annoyance that Prince Stolonov had tried to reach him, twice. So the old boy had heard the news already. Or was he calling about the protests over his plans for the tower? Wearily, Charles called him back.

'Charles! I have been trying to reach you.'

'I saw.'

'Do you know what's been going on at Anastasia's school?'

'The tower, you mean?' Charles sighed. 'Yes, I'm afraid the woods seem to be swarming with protesters, but I shouldn't lose any sleep over it. I've heard the police are going in there tomorrow to hose them down. *And* it's been raining heavily most nights, so that should flush a lot of them out!'

'I know about all that,' the prince said impatiently. 'But I'm calling about the girls. I just picked up a message from Ansti about Edie being in some sort of trouble. Of course it's not Edie's fault.'

'Is that what Ansti says?'

'She didn't need to!' The prince sounded indignant. 'You know I think the world of that girl.'

Charles said nothing.

'Ansti says she is going to be suspended.'

'Yes,' said Charles carefully.

'It is all to do with the headmistress being absent. The deputy is a vindictive woman, and poor Edie—'

'Stolly, I don't know what nonsense your daughter has told you but the facts of the matter are these – Edie was caught red-handed in the Drunken Duck ordering a cherry brandy. Anastasia was also in the vicinity, having followed Edie in to persuade her out.'

Pause. Then – 'What is this Drunken Duck? It sounds disgusting.'

'It is a pub, in the nearby village of W——. A more attentive father might have noted its existence.'

'Are you calling me an inattentive father?'

'No,' said Charles. 'On reflection I see the madness of any such slur. But it is odd, in a way, that you've never noticed the name of the hostelry local to Knight's Haddon – especially now that you own the surrounding woods.'

The prince snorted. 'Why would I notice a pub? I have no interest in these places.'

'Why indeed?' said Charles. 'And I suspect little Ansti shares your aversion. Edie on the other hand—'

'What other hand? First you say the hand is red, now you tell me it is other. I do not believe in these hands. The child is clearly innocent. Ansti said that Edie was simply following another girl, wanting to keep this other girl out of trouble.'

'What other girl?'

'In the message, she has no name.'

Charles felt unaccountably tired. 'Surely Edie would have mentioned this other girl—' he began, but the rest of his words were swallowed by a yawn. Where was his lunch, dammit! The service in the Drunken Duck was unspeakable.

'But of course, Edie will not say anything to get herself out of trouble,' the prince continued. 'It is your twisted English honour, Charles. You know what I think about that!'

Charles was silent. This was an old subject between him and Stolly.

The prince, meanwhile, was suddenly suspicious. 'Charles!'

'Stolly?'

'Is it possible you have spoken to Edie already?'

'I've tried.'

'On the telephone?'

'No. In the flesh.'

'It's not possible! You have been to the school. Oh, Charles! What did you find out about this nonsensical trip to the Tight Turtledove?'

'The facts had already been established. By the deputy dragon. Edie herself was rather . . . unresponsive.'

'You've never known how to handle her.'

'Steady on, Stoll. I invented her.'

'That is true. But you do not appreciate your invention. Did you at least persuade the dragon not to suspend her?'

'I'm afraid the boot was on the other foot. The dragon persuaded me to take her away.'

'So where is she now?'

'On a bench, outside the Alcoholic Pigeon. I was going to have a spot of lunch, and then take her to stay with her grandmother.'

'With Babka! It's not possible.'

'It's all set up.'

'You are treating her like Fanny Price!' exclaimed Stolly, who read the novels of Jane Austen once a year.

'The thing is Stolly, my lunch has arrived, at last – and if you don't mind—'

'And what is Edie having for lunch?'

'She didn't want any.'

'I must talk to her!' exclaimed Stolly. 'Charles, you are to go outside at once and give me to her. I shall tell her that she is coming to stay with me until further notice.'

'I really don't think—'

'Your thoughts do not matter to me. Your cousin does. Just do it, Charles.'

Charles was amused into obedience. In truth he was not averse to surprising Edie with some welcome news.

'Excuse me, Sir, what about your lunch?' asked a flustered waiter, as he stepped outside.

'I'll be back for it,' Charles replied.

Janet Unmasked

Edie sat on the bench, staring listlessly at the village playground, swamped by the week's rain. She had left her coat in the car, and could feel the sodden seat soaking through her skirt – but the cold without was nothing to the cold within. She thought about Cousin Charles's sly expression when he had told her that the prince was paying her fees, and hated him for it, but the person she felt angriest with was Miss Fotheringay. Why hadn't she told her the truth?

She thrust her hands into her pocket, and feeling the five-pound note that Cousin Charles had just given her, got up and stomped towards the village shop. But as she crossed the lane, she saw someone enter the churchyard, on whom she fixed in sudden interest, struck by the familiar hooded coat – and as the figure turned to shut the gate her suspicion was confirmed. It was Janet.

'Hey, Janet!' she called – but Janet didn't stop.

On an impulse Edie followed her though the gate, calling her name as she ran down the narrow path that wove between the gravestones.

'Janet! Janet, come back!' But the girl had vanished as silently as she had come.

Edie found herself running about, looking behind the tombs and the yew trees, like a child in a game of hide-and-seek – but then her eye was caught by something further off, and with a fright she saw that Janet had left the churchyard and was halfway across the field beyond. Edie supposed she must have vaulted the wall, and though the ground was steep she was going at a run.

Edie watched until she had slipped out of sight, then turned back towards the shop. But her thoughts followed the fleeing figure on the hill. She remembered Janet's appeal to her in the pub: *Do you want to help? Do you want to be part of something larger than your stupid little world at Knight's Haddon?*

The police were due to clear the woods today – that's what Janet had said. Edie looked back across the fields. She was in no doubt where Janet had gone.

And Janet was right, Edie thought now, they *should* protect the woods. So what if Miss Fotheringay had declared it out of bounds? Edie had been a coward. She'd prided herself on having a sense of justice and fair play – but her fighting spirit had only ever been roused by the petty politics of school. She thought of her mother, a journalist, who had died in pursuit of a story, and of Babka, blind but still free-spirited, and felt a rush of shame. What would they think of Edie now – feebly standing back while the woods were sliced away?

Janet was different, Edie thought grudgingly. *She* was brave.

As she walked back past the pub she imagined Cousin Charles looking for her from one of the beaded windows and quickly crossed to the other side of the lane.

When she reached the shop she saw two old jeeps parked outside, covered with stickers advertising the protest. There were people milling beside them, several of whom she recognized from the horse fair, and from the meeting yesterday morning in the pub. Then she noticed the boy with orange hair half frowning at her, as if trying to remember who she was.

Edie looked at him nervously. 'I'm going to the protest,' she heard herself saying. 'Can I come with you? I – I'm a friend of Janet – I mean, Josie,' she stumbled on, seeing his puzzled expression.

The boy smiled. 'Sure, we've got room in the truck,' he said. 'But are you coming dressed like that?'

Edie looked down at herself in dismay. For a moment she had forgotten that she was dressed in her brown Knight's Haddon tunic and yellow shirt. The uniform was like a second skin to her during term time, but now she felt like the only person to have turned up to a party in fancy dress. And to her embarrassment she saw that she was still wearing a blue 'Books Monitor' badge that the librarian had awarded her last term. She moved her fingers down her tunic and pulled the badge off. She wasn't a book monitor any more.

'Haven't you got a coat?' the boy asked.

Edie glanced back in frustration at Cousin Charles's car, which was parked down the lane. It was not only her coat that she had left in it, but also a bag with a change of clothes. Edie hadn't been allowed back into the dormitory – Matron had packed for her – but it would surely at least contain a pair of jeans.

If only she could get at it – but the car was locked, and an instinct told her it would be madness to go back to the pub and ask Cousin Charles for the key. He distrusted everyone, and was always on the lookout for the hidden motive. Meanwhile she had only the uniform she stood up in, and the five-pound note in her tunic pocket.

'You can borrow a coat off us,' the boy said. 'I'm River, by the way.'

'Edie,' Edie said.

'We'll be off soon, we're just picking up some supplies,' River said, rolling a cigarette.

'I've got money,' Edie said eagerly.

River snorted. 'You don't need to buy anything!' he said. 'We help ourselves.'

'You mean – *stealing*!' Edie whispered.

River laughed. 'Not stealing, skipping,' he said, and led Edie to the back of the shop, where some other boys were rummaging through the dustbins.

Edie watched as they pulled out unopened loaves of sliced bread, and cakes and crisps and vegetables, their wrappings still sealed.

'Best before yesterday!' one of them said, examining the labels and holding up a fruitcake in triumph.

'Sell-by dates are a capitalist conspiracy,' River explained. 'It's all a con to get people to buy more food. Didn't you know that half the food you find in dustbins is still perfectly OK to eat?'

The others clearly agreed, and were already feasting on foraged packets of hummus and pitta.

Edie wondered what the Knight's Haddon girls would make of 'skipping'. There was no tuck shop in the school, so at weekends the shop always did a brisk trade – but somehow Edie couldn't imagine Anastasia scavenging from the dustbins.

'Find any batteries?' River asked.

'Course not. Go and buy some.'

'What with?'

'River's like the Queen. He don't carry money.'

'Fair enough,' River replied good-naturedly.

'I'll buy you some batteries!' Edie volunteered, and this time River didn't protest.

She went inside, and soon found what she was looking for, but as she paid she noticed the shopkeeper, Mrs Harris, looking at her inquisitively.

'Anything else, dear?' she asked, nodding at the sweet counter as she handed Edie her change.

Edie shook her head.

'They don't usually let you out on a Sunday. Special occasion, is it?'

Edie wriggled, hating the brown uniform that she now felt branded her as a runaway. 'Yes, a very special occasion,' she said suddenly, as an impulse seized her.

As she spoke she heard the doors of the trucks slamming, and the sound of engines being coaxed to life. She thought of Knight's Haddon, of the registers and the bells, bells for everything, and the girls – girls everywhere, watching, whispering – and the maths tests on Mondays and the Latin tests on Wednesdays, and the drawer checks and the bath rota, and the freezing corridors and the closed doors; then she thought of the protest in the woods, and felt a thrilled sense of being part of something real.

'I'm not at Knight's Haddon any more,' she said, with elation in her voice. 'I'm free. Free at last!'

The others were already on board the jeeps. The first had just pulled out into the road, and Edie watched in a new agony of suspense, wondering if she was too late.

But then the driver's window in the second jeep slid open and a man leant out, his hand resting on the steering wheel. 'You Josie's mate? Jump on board,' he said, jerking his thumb towards the back.

The rear windows were lined with what looked like black bin bags, and Edie could not see inside. She climbed in blindly, to find herself in a hot, fuggy interior, squished on a seat next to River. There were two more boys on the other side of him, both dressed in camouflage jackets, and an older, wild-looking woman in the front seat with a bright turban and beads twined through a tangle of grey hair. There was something in her face that made Edie think of Miss Fotheringay – the wide, weathered eyes, the searching look.

'Panda Lily Rising Flower,' the woman said in a slow, low voice, and stretched out a hand. 'And this is Singing Hawk,' she said, stroking the driver's arm.

The driver smiled, and as the car pulled into the sunlight he slipped on a pair of heart-shaped sunglasses with a scarlet frame.

'Oh my God! Where did you get those?' Panda Lily Rising Flower shrieked, collapsing in a choke of giggles.

'Skipped!' Singing Hawk replied, punching a fist in the air.

The boys on the seat next to Edie whooped approval and then, as if to live up to his name, Singing Hawk tipped back his head and started making wild, musical chanting noises with his tongue.

The boys joined in with whistles and shouts, while Panda Lily Rising Flower threw back her head and began humming at the car ceiling. Her eyes were closed and her palms raised out, as if she had been transported into a world of her own.

Then Edie felt something wet touch her neck, and she looked round in fright to see a forlorn-looking grey dog looking at her down a drooling nose.

'So how d'you know Josie?' River asked.

'We're at school together,' Edie replied, thinking how childish it sounded. 'Or, at least, we were, but . . . I – I've just got chucked out,' she went on, hoping it might break the ice. As she spoke the car swung round a corner, and the boy leant into her, pressing her against the door.

'Chucked out? Nice one,' River said, whistling

through his teeth. 'How d'you manage that?'

'I was caught buying cherry brandies,' Edie confessed.

Everyone laughed. 'Cherry brandies! Good for you.'

'Why . . . do you all have such unusual names?' Edie asked shyly.

'Respect. For the Native Americans. They know bad stuff happens when you mess with forest energy.'

Edie felt panic rising. But she nodded sagely as though she couldn't agree more.

'Those two are Sandy Moon and Long Journey,' he explained, pointing at the two boys to his left who were busily tugging things out of a rucksack.

'Hi,' Edie said shyly – as Long Journey gave her a high-five.

'Cherry brandy, nice one!' he said.

'Yeah, my grandmother put me on to them – she drinks them all the time,' Edie replied, encouraged that her disgrace in the pub appeared to have earned her some street cred. 'Bit sweet for me. I prefer beer,' she added quickly.

'Nah, cherry brandy's cool,' Sandy Moon grinned. Then, 'Here, have this,' he said, magicking a green anorak from the floor.

Edie wriggled into it gratefully, pleased to hide her uniform. As she pulled it down she felt something bulky dig into her hip and she reached her hand into the pocket to find a turnip.

'What's this for?' she asked.

'For feeding the pigs,' River replied with a laugh. 'You know, the police – we throw them at 'em. You never been to a demo before?' Then, 'What about your friend Josie?' he asked, before Edie could answer. 'She managed to get herself chucked out of school yet too?'

Edie thought of Janet crossing the fields towards the woods. What would the Man say if she found out where she had gone? 'No,' she replied. 'Not yet.'

River whistled. 'Poor kid. She'll find a way.'

'This might be her day,' the driver said, winking at Edie in his mirror.

'What – is she coming and all?' River asked.

'Said she would be,' he replied vaguely. 'Said she'd meet us down there, I think, so long as she can escape her gaolers. Don't know what she's doing for a lift though.'

'She's walking. I saw her just a few minutes ago,' Edie said.

River looked at her but his eyes were somewhere else. 'Oh yeah?' he said absently. Janet's whereabouts were clearly not his main concern.

But Edie was puzzled. Janet had been setting off in one direction, but they seemed to be going in another. She wondered if they were nearly there. She felt disorientated not being able to see out of the windows. Just then the jeep turned and accelerated, and when she peered out of the front windscreen Edie saw that they were on a main road. But nothing looked familiar.

'Is this the right way?' she asked. The tower was only a mile from the village by the road, but it felt as if they had been driving for much longer.

'The police have closed all the roads out of the bottom

end of the village,' Singing Hawk said, slapping the wheel impatiently. 'That's why we're having to go the long way round.'

'But – aren't we going to the tower?' Edie asked.

'The tower?' The driver sounded surprised. 'Didn't you know? The protest's moved to Hayford now – that's where they're going to start building the new road into the wood. If we can only stop the road being built, then they won't be able to get any building materials to the tower, and the whole thing will have to be scotched.'

Edie frowned. Hayford was a village on the furthest side of Mesmere Wood. Edie thought of Janet's hopeless sense of direction, and wondered if she would find it. She would have to cut through the woods – but once you were inside them, every path looked the same. Edie had walked to Hayford once during an *exeat* with Miss Fotheringay, and even Fothy had got muddled trying to find the footbridge across the river.

'Does Janet – sorry, Josie – know that the protest's moved?' Edie asked anxiously.

'Dunno. But if she doesn't she'll soon work it out,' River said, pulling a spotted balaclava over his head.

'But – but *how* will she work it out?' Edie insisted. 'I mean, if she arrives at the wrong side of the woods and everyone's gone, then . . .'

She stopped. She could see that none of the others were remotely concerned whether Janet found the protest or not. But she noticed that Panda Lily Rising Flower had lowered her palms and turned from the front seat to stare at Edie with black, mascaraed eyes.

Then – 'You shouldn't have let her come,' she said solemnly, turning back to the front.

'Oh, come on, Dora – Panda, what's it matter,' Singing Hawk protested – but Panda Lily Rising Flower had started humming again.

'They might not open fire so fast if they know we've got two Knight's Haddon girls as hostages,' River said, playing with a penknife.

'Hostages?' Edie said, startled.

River smiled. 'Only kidding.'

But Sandy Moon suddenly looked serious. 'We should tip her out. Panda's right. This isn't a place for school-girls.'

Edie felt a stab of defiance. She couldn't let them tip her out – not now, not when the adventure was about to begin! And besides, where would she go? Knight's Haddon was closed to her – and she would sooner be flung in prison than have to face Cousin Charles, who by now would probably be prowling about the village, furious to discover she had strayed from her freezing billet outside the Drunken Duck.

'I'm *not* a schoolgirl,' she said fiercely. 'I just told you, I got kicked out. And – anyway, I was at the meeting in the pub yesterday. Everyone was saying you needed more people. Well, if Josie brings you more people – what . . . what's wrong with that?' she demanded.

But at that moment the truck lurched sharply to the right.

'Oi, watch it!' Singing Hawk shouted, honking his horn.

Edie yelped as all three boys were flung against her. When the truck steadied River reached over her lap and tweaked back the black plastic stuck to the window to reveal a police car spinning past on the other side of the road.

Edie looked out and caught a glimpse of the blackness of the woods, and then a whirling search-light, before River replaced the black plastic.

'Looks like we're late,' he said, smiling.

The Rule of Law

'Oh, Anastasia . . . I can't see you now. You'd better come back this afternoon,' said Miss Mannering to the pupil she found waiting outside her office. The deputy was in outdoor clothes, and wore a flustered look in contrast to her usual air of dogmatic severity.

Anastasia felt bold enough to ask after Edie. 'Are you sending her away? Because if so—'

'Yes?'

Anastasia reddened. 'She shouldn't be in trouble. It's not fair.'

'Are you saying, Anastasia, that she was forced by circumstances beyond her control into the ordering of two cherry brandies?'

'Yes . . .' said Anastasia. 'Yes, that is what I'm saying. You see . . .' She hesitated. It was impossible to explain anything without breaking her promise to Edie.

'No,' said the Man. 'I don't see. What's more, I am bored of looking.' Just then the telephone rang inside her office and she moved swiftly to pick it up, leaving the door ajar. 'Miss Pickering, ah. Thank you for ringing back. I just wanted to check that—' The Man paused and chewed her lip. 'Oh. That shouldn't have happened. No, it isn't what I arranged. I thought her aunt was coming to pick her up. Someone should have— Oh well, can't be helped.'

The deputy headmistress stood with her shoulders hunched, clenching and unclenching her fists, then looked up with a start, seeming to recall Anastasia's presence at the door.

'For heaven's sake have you no manners?' she called out, glaring at her with the receiver tucked under her chin. 'No, no, Pickering, I'm not talking to you,' she continued impatiently. 'Now close the door, child, and go away.'

Anastasia hurried off, frustrated.

Why hadn't Edie let them tell the Man that they had gone into the pub because they were worried about Newgirl? *If Edie was* really *worried about Janet*, thought Anastasia, *then surely it was her duty to inform the teachers?* But with Edie it was never that simple. It was almost a philosophy with her, that you should sort out every problem by yourself.

She and Anastasia had often disagreed about it.

'But sometimes you have to trust grown-ups—' Anastasia would argue.

'You can trust them – but it's still better not to depend on them,' Edie would say. And whatever the argument, Edie always won.

'Papa thinks you should be a lawyer when you grow up,' Anastasia said once.

'But that *is* what I'm going to be!' Edie had replied happily.

Anastasia made her way towards the san, where she assumed that Edie had been sent. Knight's Haddon wasn't called the strictest school in England for nothing, and the sanatorium was more often used for the purposes of solitary confinement than for the nursing of sick children.

She hesitated outside the door. She remembered how she had cajoled Matron into letting her in the last time Edie had been isolated there, in their first term when—

Anastasia gave herself a shake. She wouldn't think about the things that had happened then. Papa had said she didn't have to. '*The past dies if you don't poke it,*' he'd said. And now here was the Man, approaching the san with her signature thumping tread.

Coming to torture Edie with more questions, Anastasia thought grimly, as she dived down a staircase. Where now? She had no desire to see any of the other girls. And as for Janet – Anastasia did not trust herself to set eyes on her without lashing out.

If only Fothy would come back! *She* would believe Edie was innocent, even if no one else did. *And I will never tease Edie about Fothy again*, Anastasia resolved guiltily. She heard the lunch bell clanging from the East

Tower, but she could not face the dining room, and the table full of questioning faces.

She ducked into a deserted corridor and meandered towards the West Tower, then found her steps leading her outside, towards the animal house. It had a desolate feel for her now, with Precious and Treasure's cage standing empty, its mesh door hanging open. And yet, since the ferrets' release, she found she was often drawn there.

Sometimes she just stood in the doorway, waiting for them to come back.

Spots of rain began to fall and Anastasia slipped quickly into the animal house, out of the wet. The door was divided in two parts, like a stable, but when she tried to pull shut the lower section she felt something tugging on the other side – and looked up with a start to see a tall bedraggled man in a frayed tweed coat peering in at her.

'Ah!' she said, stepping back in fright.

'I'm so sorry,' said the man, smiling with a weak, distracted air. 'Please don't be alarmed. There's really no need . . . Except, I suppose, for the fact that you don't know me—'

'I do know you,' Anastasia said. 'You're the man who gave us the ferrets at the horse fair.'

He looked briefly bewildered. Then, 'Ah-ha . . . the ferrets!' he said, smiling. 'Now you're talking! What happened to the ferrets, eh? I don't think I ever heard.'

'I don't know. They used to live in here,' Anastasia said primly, gesturing at the dank interior behind her and pointing to the empty cage in the corner. 'Someone let them out.'

'Let them out, eh?' said the ferret man. 'Someone did that?' He seemed sad for a moment. Then, 'Ah well, they'll be all right. They're native you know. They'll be fine in the wild. Better all round.'

Anastasia hated him. Why did no one care about Precious and Treasure except her? 'What do you want?' she asked, hearing – and hating – the nervous hoarseness in her voice.

'I've come to see someone. Girl called Josie. I need to find her, it's . . .' The man looked at her, hesitantly – but with a flicker of conspiracy in his face: 'You know what's happening at the woods today?'

Anastasia knew perfectly well. But she shook her head, looking at him suspiciously.

'Sorry,' said the ferret man. 'Not Josie – I mean, Janet. Janet Stone. Friend of yours?'

'I know her,' Anastasia said guardedly. 'Why?'

'Got to find her . . . this protest, you see . . . the protest in the woods . . . she wrote to say not to bother, coming up here. She'd be there. But I don't like it. It's a bad business, what they're doing . . .'

Anastasia looked at him sharply, as suddenly his slurred speech made sense. He had come to the school to spirit Janet away to the protest! He must be one of the people Newgirl had met yesterday in the pub.

'I might be able to find her,' she said, playing for time as a daring plan took shape. For if she could only detain him, then Janet's plan would be exposed without

Anastasia having to tell any tales as such. 'Would you like me to bring her here?' she asked politely, standing back from the door with a tiny flourish of her hand, gesturing him to come inside.

'That would be . . . dandy,' he replied, advancing into the shed with an uncertain gait. Anastasia heard the clink of glass bottles in the carrier bag he clutched to his side. She remembered Belinda's matter-of-fact diagnosis at the horse fair: *Drunk as a skunk! Couldn't you smell it?*

This time Anastasia could, and her nostrils curled in protest.

'Now what have we here? Goodness me! It's Flopsy, Mopsy and Peter Rabbit!' the man said, gesturing at the cages as he lurched inside.

Anastasia slowly edged herself into the doorway, her eyes fixed on him intently. She knew now that what she had to do was to get out of the animal house herself, and leave him locked inside. But she was afraid that he might get wind of her plot and make a sudden run for it.

'That was the ferrets' cage, that one over there,' she said, nodding towards Precious and Treasure's old home in the corner, as her hand reached, trembling, for the door. 'I – I know someone must have let them out . . . they could never have escaped on their own . . . look how strong the wire is!'

The man grunted, and half turned his head – and as he did so Anastasia slipped outside and silently whipped shut the bottom half of the stable door, nudging the bolt across it with her knee.

She reached for the top of the door, but the wind had swung it back against the side of the shed.

The ferret man turned, and for a moment Anastasia feared he was going to rush at her – but he seemed not to have noticed that he was nearly her prisoner.

'Are you going to help me find her?' he asked, looking up at her over the bottom half of the door.

'Why? Does she want to see you?'

The man smiled. 'That's a tricky one. If you see her, tell her that Sto— No, don't tell her who I am. Just tell her there's a man come to see her about the woods. Much better. Better all round.'

Anastasia nodded. So she was right!

Then – 'There's a girl she's friendly with. Eddy, I think the name is,' he went on. 'You know her? She'll do, if you can't find my Jose— Tell her it's a message about the woods. You needn't look so suspicious, little girl. It's for their own good – both of them. There's something they need to know.'

Anastasia felt a stab of anger. It was one thing wanting to persuade Janet into the stupid protest at Mesmere Wood, but why was he so determined to get Edie involved as well? She for one wouldn't let him! Janet could go to Hell in a handcart, but Anastasia wouldn't let Edie get into any more scrapes on her behalf! With a beating heart, she leant across and reached for the upper half of the door.

'Hey, where are you going? I'll come with you,' the man said, stumbling towards her. 'Wait a minute? What are you—?'

But in a hair's breadth Anastasia had snapped the door shut and sliced back the bolt, trapping him inside.

'What's going on?'

'I've locked you in,' Anastasia replied, as she squinted in at him through the crack in the door.

'Locked me in? What – why on earth?'

'It's for your own good.'

'Wait a minute.'

'I can't. I've got to rush,' Anastasia said, skipping away with a laugh of triumph. 'It's better like this. Better all round.'

Miss Fotheringay was already running late when she encountered the police barriers. The river near the school had risen after the long nights of rain, and a huge lorry was parked across the flooded road, which was crackling with policemen and walkie-talkies.

She wound down her window, and leant her head outside. 'Has a tree fallen down?' she asked, with a nod towards the looming hill of Mesmere Woods.

'We wish,' replied an officer. 'But the tree-huggers won't let go of 'em.'

Miss Fotheringay frowned. Last week she had read that a compromise had been reached with the forest protesters, that no trees were to be destroyed until a further report had been submitted. She had assumed the protesters' camp would be disbanded. 'I thought they'd agreed a delay—'

The policeman shook his head. 'Can't agree nothing with this lot. They left by one gate and came back through another. I tell you, it's a fight they're after, and a fight they're going to get.'

Miss Fotheringay nodded. It sounded like the usual story – activists more interested in getting arrested than anything else. It was a subject she had often argued about with Edie's mother Anna.

Anna's arguments came back to her now, as the headmistress waited impatiently for the temporary lights to let her through.

– 'Of course we don't want to go to prison,' Anna had said about a peace campaign she had been involved with. 'But unjust laws are a form of violence. In which case you have to break the law, and then submit peacefully to arrest. That way you resist violence non-violently. The trouble with you, Caro, is that you're a natural-born autocrat. Therefore you have an instinctive distrust of rebellion.'

– 'Rubbish,' Miss Fotheringay had replied hotly. 'I simply believe in the Rule of Law.'

– 'So did the Fascists!'

They had enjoyed arguing with one another, reflected Miss Fotheringay, as the lights changed to green, without ever agreeing on much.

She wondered if Edith Wilson would become a firebrand like her mother. She hoped not. Janet Stone was clearly longing for adventure on the barricades, but she had an idea that Edith, though quite as brave as her mother, was more reserved by nature, slower and more reasonable in her conclusions. Or was she? Miss Fotheringay bit her lip as she considered how comparatively little she had seen of Edith this term, and how unresponsive Edith had been at their last meeting. 'You need to go carefully with that one,' her father had warned her, when he had asked after Edie from his sickbed. 'It can't be easy for her, having the headmistress as her special protector.'

'Nothing's been easy for Edith since the day she was born. She's more than a match for a few sniping school-girls,' Miss Fotheringay had replied lightly.

It was just past one when the headmistress let herself in by the heavy front door of Knight's Haddon, with a key as long as a trowel. *Lunch time*, she thought, relishing the sense of order as she swept through the empty corridors. But thinking of Anna made her restless. When she had finished work she would summon Edith to her office, Miss Fotheringay decided, remembering the cakes she had bought for tea.

Ding Dong

As Anastasia sprinted back into the school she saw Miss Fotheringay's car parked in the drive and flew straight to the West Tower to find her. But on the way she passed Miss Mannering's office and heard a commotion coming from inside: the headmistress and her deputy, their voices raised to a pitch!

Anastasia slunk back against the wall of the corridor, listening with furtive delight. The voices rose and fell, but even at their lowest they were audible – and this time it was the deputy who was receiving the rollicking:

'I don't understand.'

'I think I have been perfectly clear.'

'You have sent Edith Wilson away without consulting me. It beggars belief, Diana. There is something missing from your story.'

'The something missing is the something you have failed to pick up. I caught Edith Wilson red-handed in the Drunken Duck, ordering cherry brandies. I asked for an explanation. On receiving none I followed the usual procedure.'

'The usual procedure! There is no usual procedure as far as Edith is concerned!'

'That, perhaps, is the problem I wish to address,' said Miss Mannering quietly.

'There is no problem, and you had no business addressing it.'

'You are not making sense, Caroline. Listen to me! I wish no harm to Edith, why would I? But I cannot stand by and witness the harm that is being done to her. You know that Knight's Haddon is the best – the only – chance she has ever had of a normal childhood. Why are you doing your best to derail it?'

'That's not fair!'

'Not fair is the charge that is being thrown at Edith Wilson, daily,' Miss Mannering snapped. 'Not fair is the charge I wished to avoid in this instance by treating her just as I would treat anyone else.'

'The point is, Diana, that Edith must have been in the pub for a good reason.'

'That may be, but since she wouldn't tell me what it was I took the decision to send her home—'

'You know perfectly well, Diana, that Edith Wilson has no home outside this school.'

'Nonsense. She has a guardian and it was with her that I was in touch.'

Just then the argument was interrupted by the ring of a phone. There was silence in the room, broken after a few minutes by the Man, speaking in a voice quite different from the defensive tone she had used previously: 'It would appear that Edith has given Mr Rodriguez the slip.'

Anastasia stiffened. So Edie had been sent away – and then done a runner! Anastasia remembered the gleam in Edie's eye when Janet had tried to persuade her to sneak off to the woods. That is where she would have gone.

'Facts, Diana, I need facts,' Miss Fotheringay urged.

'I don't have very many,' Miss Mannering replied tersely. 'But it seems that after picking Edie up, Mr Rodriguez stopped for lunch at the Drunken Duck.'

'The Drunken Duck! Again! Why is everyone so determined to lure the poor child into that dingy place!'

'Edith did not, apparently, accompany him into the premises. He left her sitting on the bench outside—'

'Left her outside – *in the dead of winter*?'

'And when he left the pub half an hour later,' Miss Mannering continued, her voice rising over this interruption, 'Edith was not there.'

'Then where the hell is she?'

'That is what we shall endeavour to find out. Mr Rodriguez is on his way here now—'

'*On his way here?* What good will that do? Why isn't he looking for her in the village? Has he called the police?'

Anastasia stiffened. Janet had said the police were going to arrest people at the protest. Would they arrest Edie too – for running away, or ordering cherry brandies in the pub? She remembered an afternoon in Moscow, long ago, when her father had caught her in his study, stealing peppermints from his drawer. '*If you steal, the police will come,*' he had said to her, his eyes grave. '*When the police take you away, you never come back . . .*' She had an image of Edie being carted away in hand-cuffs, in the back of a speeding car.

But the voices railed on from inside the study – 'If he didn't call the police, then call them yourself!'

'No!' Anastasia cried, as the two mistresses turned on her in astonishment. 'Don't! Not the police! I know where Edie must have gone – she's gone to the woods! To join the protest! But it was Janet's idea, not Edie's. Please, I can tell you everything. You see . . . it – it was because of Janet that Edie went into the pub!'

Miss Mannering made to say something, but Miss Fotheringay silenced her with a look. 'Explain yourself, Anastasia,' the headmistress said coolly.

And so Anastasia found herself hurriedly relating the story that she had promised Edie she wouldn't tell – about how they had discovered Janet's involvement with the protesters when they had slunk after her into the pub.

'Edie only ordered a cherry brandy because – because she thought that's the sort of thing people do!' Anastasia finished in a breathless rush. Then she remembered her prisoner. 'If you don't believe me, I can prove it! There's a witness! He came to get them, to take them to the woods. He's the one who's put them up to it. And – and you can go and talk to him,' she went on, wishing her story didn't sound quite so far-fetched.

Miss Mannering snorted. 'What on earth do you mean? Who came to get them?'

'I – I don't know exactly,' Anastasia answered truthfully. 'Just that he—'

'*He?* He who?' Miss Mannering barked.

'He came to the school!' Anastasia said impatiently. 'And I think he's one of the protesters. He didn't make much sense, but he knew all about Janet wanting to be at the protest – that's where she's been sloping off to, when she goes off on her own.'

'*Goes off on her own?*' The Man's eyes bulged.

Anastasia nodded. 'Yes, you know, on Saturdays – she never waits for a walking partner to go to the village, she always just signs herself out then runs off on her own without letting anyone catch up—'

'On her *own?*' The Man looked aghast.

'Yes, I . . . I mean—' Anastasia came to a blushing stop. Talk about sneaking!

'It's all right, Anastasia, you are not going to get Janet into any more trouble than she is in already,' Miss Fotheringay said calmly, addressing her pupil's anxieties as if she had spoken them out loud. 'But talk clearly, and tell us everything you know. Who is this man? Where did you see him?'

Anastasia nodded, as she tried to master her thoughts. 'I saw him just now, up by the animal house. I was there, you know, I often go there, to see if Precious and Treasure – my ferrets – have come back. And – and there he was! The man who gave us the ferrets at the horse fair!'

'Wait a minute,' said Miss Fotheringay. 'I thought you

bought the ferrets.'

'N-no. Not exactly. There was this man and he wanted . . . oh, I don't know what he wanted! But now he's come to take Janet away to the protest—'

'Hmm,' said the Man, chewing her lip. 'No chance of that. I happen to know she's gone with the lacrosse team to Rousham Heights for the Under-Thirteen A-squad inter-season Open Cup Skipper Shield semi-finals.'

Miss Fotheringay looked at her in surprise. 'Since when has Janet been in the lacrosse team?' she asked sharply.

'She *hates* lacrosse!' Anastasia joined in effusively.

'Well—' Miss Mannering looked defensive. 'I passed her this morning on her way outside and naturally enquired as to where she was going and that is what she told me.'

'I see,' Miss Fotheringay said slowly. 'And you believed her?'

Miss Mannering did not reply.

'And was she carrying a lacrosse stick?' Miss Fotheringay asked.

No answer.

'Well, it looks like Janet has fooled us all,' Miss Fotheringay concluded briskly. 'We are now missing two girls – Janet and Edith. And from what Anastasia tells us they have run away to the woods with a mystery man—'

'No!' Anastasia cried. 'No . . . no, you see, they can't have done. That's . . . that's what he wanted – he wanted them to go with him to the protest, that's why he came

here – to fetch them! But I stopped him, you see . . . I
. . .' She looked at the mistresses doubtfully: *'I've locked
him up!'*

As the door of the animal house closed on Anastasia's
prisoner, Janet Stone was running purposefully through
the woods.

She wondered if anyone at the school had noticed yet
that she had gone. Had the Man rumbled her story
about lacrosse and sent out a search party to track her
down – a pack of thirsty, baying bloodhounds, recruited
from her spiritless staff?

Janet glanced back over her shoulder, relishing the
thrill of escape. Let them come after her with their rule-
books and their detentions and their pointless bells! By
the time they caught up with her, it would be too late.
One thing was certain: after the stunt that Janet had
planned for this afternoon, Knight's Haddon would
never take her back.

She had had no contact with the protesters since
yesterday's meeting in the pub – it was hateful having
no mobile phone, so not being able to receive the rapid
flurry of updates and coded alerts. But Janet knew what
to do. Everything had been explained to her. She knew
she had to hurry. She looked at her watch, and started to
run. It was nearly two o'clock. She had to reach the
camp before the police arrived, or the whole escapade
would fail.

But she was struck by the stillness in the woods. The
protest should have reached its pitch – at yesterday's

meeting, they'd said that more than two hundred people had pledged to come and try and keep the police at bay. Operation Dunsinane promised to be something big. But there was an eerie silence – and when she finally arrived at the camp, all but one of the tents had gone, and the fires had almost burnt out.

Janet looked around her, bewildered. She could just make out the outline of the tower through the trees – before, there had been protesters camped all around it, with their fires and lanterns, but now everyone was gone, everything was dark. Surely they hadn't given up?

Then she remembered her whispered conversation with Angel in the pub. *'They won't crack Dunsinane. We're going to take them by surprise! The police won't know what's coming!'*

So that was it, Janet thought, gleeful. Everyone was hiding, ready to rush out when the police moved in. Janet wondered if she should try to find the others before carrying out her stunt – then thought better of it. They'd come back soon enough – and when they did she could surprise them. And wow, they'd be impressed! Sometimes Janet had sensed that the protesters didn't take her seriously – they'd seemed grateful enough for the food she'd stolen from the Knight's Haddon kitchens and sneaked up to the wood in a wheelbarrow. But she knew that when her back was turned they mocked her for belonging to such a stupid school. Now she'd show them what she was made of!

Janet slipped her rucksack from her back and took out the long, metal lock that she had smuggled from

Folly Farm. The suffragettes had chained themselves to the railings outside the Houses of Parliament, so why shouldn't Janet chain herself to a tree? That would stop the bulldozers tearing down the woods!

She remembered the headmistress's scathing tone as she stood in front of the class, moulding the events of history according to her own, poisoned prejudice:

'The suffragettes achieved nothing then, just as activists seldom achieve anything now. Their cause may be right, but their methods are potty.'

Janet recoiled at the memory. Deeds, not words! She would teach Fothy not to mock the activists' cause. She looked around her hurriedly, searching for a tree that would suit her purpose. The protesters had shown her the route that the new road was going to take – along the side of the river, then through the woods to the tower. But the trees around her were all too thick – the lock would never fit round the trunks.

She ran on, her long legs taking her rapidly across the rickety footbridge, following where the road was supposed to go, looking for something to which she could attach herself – then down near the river's bank she saw a cluster of white trees, with trunks as slim as lamp posts.

The river had risen, and it was rushing forwards, lashing over on the rocks. But her brain was racing, and she hardly heard the heavy thunder of water as she tossed her rucksack into the bushes and scrambled on, up to the trees. Instead, scenes from her first torrid term at Knight's Haddon came flashing back. She thought with misery of the ferrets, and of Anastasia – and then of Edie, who was the only thing from that horrid place that Janet would be sorry to lose.

As she pulled herself up against a tree beside the water she heard an echo of Edie's voice: '*What I don't get is why you're so desperate to leave school when you hate home. If you succeed in getting chucked out of Knight's Haddon, you'll have to live with one of your parents. Wouldn't that be worse?*'

Janet blinked the thought away. She would hate to live with either of her parents – with her mother, who always seemed irritated by her, or her pathetic father, who always looked to Janet to prop him up, and put things right.

But it wouldn't come to that. She'd save the woods, and then she'd find another cause, somewhere else where she was needed.

She remembered Anastasia's angry words to Edie in the pub: '*Janet doesn't care about the woods. You know what her game is. She just wants to get sent home.*'

Janet smiled. It was true, she did want to get herself expelled, and now she would.

But she was doing it for the woods too. *They are beautiful woods*, she thought, as she pushed her spectacles up her nose, and placed the D-lock round her neck. She heard the cautioning roar of the water, and felt a freezing spray sting her cheeks, but turned her face away. *They are beautiful woods.* She snapped the lock shut. *The woods are beautiful . . . the woods are worth saving . . .*

A Lock Without a Key

Edie sat squashed in the back seat as the truck rattled on, faster and faster. The dog had started to bark, and she could hear sirens shrieking. Then they swerved off the road and started careering down a rough track into the forest, with trees enclosing them tightly on either side.

'*Buoung – buoung – buong!*' Panda Lily Rising Star chanted in a trance-like voice, clutching her hands to the dashboard.

'*Buoung – buoung – buoung!*' chorused the boys, as the truck bounced on, lurching from side to side like a wind-battered ship.

Edie felt sick. She closed her eyes, and when she opened them again she saw a man waving at them in the grass ahead, with a turkey clutched in his arms:

'*Stop!*' she shrieked, for they were heading straight at him – then the truck braked so violently she was flung against the front seat.

The boys leapt out with a cheer, and when Edie followed she found herself in a small forest clearing, full of make-shift tents and shelters made from sheets of corrugated iron covered with plastic sheeting. Running round the edge of the camp was a fence of barbed wire.

There was a purposeful mood, with people everywhere, shouting to each other and hauling things out of cars and trailers, while dogs scavenged around the campfires.

A group of men had gathered around Singing Hawk, and were helping him unload boxes from the back of his truck, while Panda Lily Rising Flower had wandered into the crowd, humming, with her palms raised up to heaven.

'Hey, Panda! Did you remember to get some milk?' someone shouted, as Panda Lily Rising Flower floated past a mud-splattered caravan, her skirt trailing on the ground.

Edie looked around her anxiously. The camp seemed well hidden, with woods closing blackly on every side. She wondered how Janet would ever find it – her sense of direction was confused enough at best. But surely *someone* must have seen her that morning, and told her which way to go – or offered her a lift? Edie recognized several faces from yesterday's meeting in the pub, but when she started making enquiries, no one seemed to care.

'Janet? Sorry.'

'Josie? She the one from the school? Dunno, haven't seen her. But she said yesterday she'd try and pitch up.'

'Headmistress has probably locked her in,' someone laughed.

Edie was aware of the action notching up around her. People had started running, shouting, then she heard a noise from the woods, an explosion of some kind, followed by the sound of more sirens shrieking.

'What's happened?' Edie asked.

'Bulldozers are coming in,' someone said.

Edie felt fear rising in her gullet. She could see that a missing schoolgirl was the last thing on anyone's mind. She looked for River, but couldn't find him. Then she spotted some other boys she recognized from the meeting in the pub and ran over to them breathlessly.

'I'm looking for Janet – Josie!' she explained hurriedly. 'She's . . . she should be here, but . . . I'm worried she's lost—'

'That the girl from the meeting?' one of them asked. 'She's probably gone to the old place.'

'What do you mean? Where—'

The boy shrugged. 'I sent out text messages to everyone this morning saying the camp'd moved. Maybe she didn't check her phone.'

'*Check her phone!*' Edie almost shrieked. 'She hasn't got a phone!'

'Don't worry, she'll catch up soon enough,' another boy said. 'Last place was only a mile away.'

'Yeah, and she'll turn round soon enough – the river's flooding.'

Another boy whistled through his teeth. 'Looks like we cleared out our stuff just in time.'

'Yeah, they reckon the bridge will be swept away if the water rises any further—'

'*Flooded?* What do you mean?' Edie asked sharply.

The boy looked at her quizzically. 'Where've you been? It's only been raining for six nights solid – hadn't you noticed?'

Edie frowned. Of course she had noticed the rain, and the sodden lacrosse pitches around the school – but she had not thought of its implications beyond Knight's Haddon.

'All the roads through the valley are flooded,' another boy said. 'All the fields down below Hayford are under water. If it gets any worse the dam will break.'

'Yeah, and guess who the police are gonna blame for it!'

Edie gazed at them stupidly. 'But . . . but Janet—' She looked up to see River had appeared.

'Don't look so worried, Knight's Haddon, she'll be fine,' he said.

'She might not be,' Edie said in a choked voice, but everyone was looking away from her, towards the sound of a crash somewhere deep in the forest.

Edie looked too, but her vision was blurred by the terrifying scenes her mind threw before her. When she had walked through the woods with Miss Fotheringay the previous year the river had been swollen by days of rain, and Edie remembered the din as the waters rushed round the bend, and the hand Miss Fotheringay had offered her as they crossed the bridge near the tower, with the current crashing beneath them, touching their faces with its spray.

Miss Fotheringay had not spoken as they had crossed the bridge, and Edie wondered if she had been afraid. It was only later that the headmistress had told Edie of the time when the dam that stood a few hundred metres upriver from the tower had broken, and the footbridge had been swept away. She had spoken quietly, as if to herself, but Edie had guessed that that was why the river was out of bounds. It did not enter the boundaries of Knight's Haddon, but it looped close to the tower, then wove along about half a mile beyond the boundary of the school park.

Edie thought of the way Janet had run across the field – furtive-looking, with her head bowed. 'We've got to find her!' she said, her voice cutting through a fever of nightmarish thoughts. 'Please, you've got to come—'

But as she spoke a whistle shrilled inside the wood. Then, 'Save Mesmere!' came the cry, and 'Save Mesmere!' came the chorus, as the camp marched as one across the clearing and into the woods – forty, fifty people, chanting and shouting, with dogs yapping at their heels.

'Wait!' Edie cried, but no one did. In minutes the camp was deserted, save for one lonely collie, howling on its chain.

Edie stared after them, then turned the other way and set off at a run.

She knew from the meeting yesterday in the pub

where the old camp was: on the other side of the woods, nearest to Knight's Haddon, and close to where the river wound past the tower.

But once she had entered the woods every direction looked the same. She stumbled on, ducking through the low branches, searching for a path or a clearing, or any familiar sign to tell her she was going the right way. But the wood was becoming thicker, and the evening was drawing in – it would soon be dark . . .

'Janet!' she shouted. 'Jan–et! Where . . . are . . . you?' But the only reply was the teasing whisper of the trees.

Edie did not know how long she had been running when she finally recognized the path that led to the bridge near the tower. She followed it, until she was nearly at the river, but then something in the undergrowth caught her eye. At first she thought it was a coat – but when she pulled it out she saw that it was a rucksack. And she recognized it even before she read the name scrawled in felt-tip pen on the shoulder straps: it was Janet's.

She at once fell to the ground and tore through the contents – a jersey, a packet of Janet's beloved strawberry liquorice bootlaces and a wallet containing two ten-pound notes and, in the coin compartment, the small silver key which she had last seen sellotaped to the back of the postcard.

Edie shovelled everything back into the bag, and peered fearfully through the trees:

'Janet! Janet – ARE YOU THE-EEEERE?'

No answer. But now Edie could see slivers of light

shimmering through the wood ahead, and she flung the rucksack on her back and ran on.

Then Edie became aware of a low rumbling sound – soft at first, and as she followed it through the trees it seemed to grow deeper and deeper, until she could feel it roaring in her ears. Suddenly the wood opened, and she saw the river rushing in front of her, but pouring in a frenzied rapid as she had never seen it before.

On the opposite bank, she could see a small clearing containing the desolate remains of a camp – several fires, still smouldering, rubbish strewn everywhere, and a collapsing tent, its canvas front flung open to reveal a clutter of tins and saucepans strewn on the sodden matting inside. The place had an eerie feeling, as if it had been abandoned in haste. But along the river's bank in front of her – where the road would run – was a makeshift barricade of flimsy poles and rope, strung out between the trees, hung with tattered green posters proclaiming the protest.

And there, in the centre of it, was Janet, standing with phantom-like stillness against the pale thin trunk of a silver birch with the water crashing by her feet.

'Janet, get down!' Edie shrieked, as she dropped the rucksack and ran towards her. 'The dam's burst! Get back, you idiot! You'll be swept away!'

But her cries were swallowed by the river's din, and it was only when Edie had almost reached her that Janet seemed to notice she was there. She said nothing, but looked at Edie with a steady gaze as she placed her hands meaningfully on the black metal loop round her neck.

Edie looked at it bewildered for a moment, until she realized what it was: the bicycle padlock.

Deeds, not words! Edie felt a feverish sweat take hold of her as she remembered Janet's outburst in Miss Fotheringay's class.

'Get down, you idiot!' she shouted, reaching up to her, and wrenching desperately at the lock. In the first moment of confusion Edie thought only of trying to break the padlock free. Then she thought of the silver key in the wallet in Janet's rucksack.

'Wait!' Edie shouted.

Janet said nothing, but her eyes were fixed on the river and gleamed with fear.

Edie turned, but was aware only of the vast, swirling mass of grey water lashing at them as it smashed over the rocks. Then she saw something moving by the river's bank. At first she could not make out what it was, but as her eyes followed it, half-dazed, she saw that it was Janet's rucksack, being whipped away by the current.

'I've really gone and done it now,' shouted Newgirl, in a show of desperate bravado. 'I've only gone and locked myself up and thrown away the key!'

A Mockery King of Snow

Anastasia's forester was slumped on the floor of the animal shed, snoring loudly.

'Oh dear,' said Miss Fotheringay. 'Oh very dear.'

'Do you recognize him?' asked Miss Mannering, officiously shining a torch in the prisoner's face.

Miss Fotheringay did not answer. The prisoner, meanwhile, shifted in his slump.

'Hello!' he said as he put out a hand against the beam. 'What's this?'

'It's a torch,' said Miss Mannering, switching it off. 'Don't move!' she added, when he made as though to right himself. 'That's an order!' she explained, unnecessarily.

The Man is actually mad, thought Anastasia. She stole a glance at Miss Fotheringay, wondering if she thought so too. But Fothy's face gave nothing away. She was staring at the prisoner, frowning.

'I know you, don't I?' said the prisoner, returning the stare.

'My name is Caroline Fotheringay.'

'Ah yes,' said the prisoner in a gloomy voice. 'Eustacia's told me all about you.'

'I understand that you have a message for your— For Janet Stone?'

'Well of course I do!' he said with sudden animation. 'That's why I'm here. My *raison d'etre*, you might almost say.'

Miss Fotheringay said nothing.

'So where is she? Where is my Jose? That one there,' – the prisoner's eyes swivelled to where Anastasia was standing, in the shadows – 'that one there promised to fetch her here.'

'I did not!' said Anastasia, indignant. 'You just assumed I would.'

'Is that right?' The prisoner shrugged gracefully. 'If she says it, then it must be true. Of course there is a school of thought—' He paused and patted the ground with his hands, as though feeling around for his scattered wits, 'It doesn't much matter what that school of thought thinks since this school isn't . . . that school. Have I got you there, ladies?'

Anastasia felt uneasy. Her prisoner was talking nonsense again, and seemed completely lacking in fight. She was reminded, suddenly, of a Shakespeare play in which the king had lost his crown and had wandered round the stage almost revelling in his misfortune.

'*For God's sake let us sit upon the ground and tell sad stories of the death of kings,*' she murmured.

'Richard II,' Miss Fotheringay said softly. '*Would that I were a mockery king of snow.*'

Anastasia glowed. Fothy understood everything. She always had.

'I'm sorry for not standing up,' the prisoner said. 'The truth is, I feel a little unwell.'

'Unwell?' queried Miss Mannering.

He looked up. 'Yes,' he said quietly. 'People tell me it's an illness and I'm beginning to think they may be right. But I'm in your way, ladies. I can see that. If one of you would be so kind as to fetch me Josie, then I could be on my way in a jiffy.'

'You'd have to stand up first,' Anastasia pointed out.

'Doesn't miss a trick this one, does she?' he said, addressing himself to Miss Fotheringay. But getting no response he turned back to Anastasia: 'When you're unwell, as I am, you have to be very careful with yourself. After a stand . . . comes a fall. Maybe.'

Anastasia found that she couldn't look at her prisoner any more. She couldn't bear to see what an unworthy adversary he had turned out to be, and she ached with something that felt like anger but wasn't. Later, she would learn to give it a name. '*For pity's sake—*' she would say, and then stop in her tracks, and know the ache for what it was.

Fothy meanwhile appeared to have found her voice, at last. 'What did you want to say to Janet Stone?'

The prisoner looked at her through narrowed eyes. 'If

I tell you that—' he began, as though embarking on a deal.

'Just tell me,' Miss Fotheringay said.

The prisoner slumped. 'She wrote to me, to tell me she was going to run away and join the protest in the forest,' he said simply. 'I've come to tell her she mustn't do it.'

'Do what?'

'They call it the D-lock protest. First it was off, then it was on again. It's going to be nasty. They're after a fight, you know, and I want Janet to stay out of it. That's an order,' he added, addressing his mournful chuckle at Miss Mannering.

But before Miss Mannering could respond to the man's impudence, Miss Fotheringay took her arm and marched her to the door. Anastasia did not hear much of the hushed exchange which followed, but noted the agitation in Fothy's tone.

Then the Man turned, and looked back at the prisoner. 'Very well, Caroline, go with Miss Pickering, and go there at once. Meanwhile I will call the groundsmen and ask them to remove this inebriated forester from the premises.'

'He's not a forester,' replied Miss Fotheringay briskly. 'He's a father.'

Edie the Liberator!

E die watched, mesmerized, as the rucksack danced out on the rushing water, the scrawled letters of Janet's name still visible on the black straps that trailed pathetically in the foam. She moved by instinct towards the bank, her hand stretched out in a futile gesture, but then a lash of water sent her reeling back.

'Edie!' Janet shrieked, her show of bravado over.

Edie scrambled back to her feet, a series of rapid calculations spinning through her mind. The village was close by – she could sprint there and raise the alarm, and get someone to come and cut Janet free. But panic had confused her sense of direction. Should she go upstream or down . . . was the road this side of the river or that? And was the footbridge even still there?

As her thoughts raged she became aware of a lull in

the roar of the water, as if the river had suddenly stopped to catch its breath. Then came a long, sunken tremor as a chunk of the dam upriver heaved open, and a vast wall of grey water reared into the air. Edie watched, transfixed, as the wave hovered before smashing forwards, flinging a twisted debris of planks and branches.

'Edie! *Help me!*' Janet screamed, writhing against the tree as the water gushed to her feet.

Edie's head turned dizzy. It was a nightmare! And any minute a bell would ring and Sally would whip back the duvet, laughing, telling her to wake up . . .

But there was no bell. There was only the endless raging of the water, and the dreadful shrill behind her as Janet screamed for help: 'Edie, Edie! I'm going to drown. The rucksack, Edie! Please, get it back!'

Edie turned helplessly. Couldn't Janet see that she could never get it back? But then she became aware of a black shape rising in front of her, and looked up to see a tree trunk caught in the debris by the bank, the rucksack tangled in the end of it.

'Edie!' Janet screamed, as Edie flung herself down the bank. 'Edie, come back!'

Edie could feel the spray pounding her, lashing her cheeks like a whip. She bowed her head and pulled herself on to the tree trunk, her hands clinging for dear life to the gnarled clumps of bark. She could feel the trunk moving beneath her, and she could see the rucksack tossing on the water ahead, caught only by a tangled strap.

As she reached ahead and seized it she heard another bewildered scream, but dared not look round. She inched backwards along the trunk, wriggling like a snake, her eyes half blinded by the spray.

As Edie finally clambered back on to the bank, Janet gave a whoop of pleasure. 'Edie the Liberator!' she cried in a gleeful voice, as Edie fished the precious silver key from the sodden wallet and stumbled back to the tree Janet was locked to.

The words stung Edie like a lash, and for a moment she froze, hearing again the taunts she had suffered for the crime she did not commit. She looked up at Newgirl, and saw only excitement in her face.

'How dare you!' Edie shouted – but Janet seemed oblivious to the pain she had stirred.

'Come on – what are you waiting for?' she cried, craning her neck impatiently. 'Unlock me before I drown!'

Edie had the key poised to the lock, but now she shrank backwards, out of Janet's reach.

'What? Edie – *for Christ's sake*! Edie—'

When Edie spoke her voice was cold and clear. 'Janet Stone. Did – you – release – the – ferrets?' she said, fixing her with a lethal stare.

'Answer me Janet. *WAS – IT – YOU?*'

'Stop it, you maniac!' Janet shouted, squirming against the tree. 'Can't you see, I'm going to die!'

Edie heard another tremor – there was more mischief in the dam yet – but still her eyes did not flinch from Janet's face. She threw up her arm, raising the key in the air, then leant closer, until their noses were almost touching. Edie looked into Janet's eyes, staring steadily through the splattered lenses of her spectacles.

'I know it was you, Janet! You thought they were yours to do what you liked with! You thought it because you're Josie, and the ferret man meant them for you! But why? Why did you let them go and let me take the rap? TELL ME NOW.'

The river crashed on behind them, but neither girl saw it, so tightly were their eyes locked.

When Janet finally spoke, her voice was even. 'I did it, Wilson, because the man you call "the ferret man" was my father. My useless father who should have stopped me being sent to school, and thought he could make everything all right with a basket of stupid ferrets. I never meant you to take the blame and I was always going to put it right, but—'

Edie believed her. It was the truth at last. She felt her chest expand as she leant forward with the key. 'Free at last,' she said, as she carefully removed the lock from Janet's neck.

Janet clung to her arm as they clambered from the bank, not stopping until they had reached the safety of the low ridge above the river.

Edie looked down at the water in triumph. They'd escaped! But she had not reckoned on the inexhaustibility of Janet Stone.

'*Come on*, Edie! Hurry up or we'll be late for the protest!' she urged, as Edie was still gasping for breath. 'They must have gone to the other side of the woods . . . there was another camp, I heard them talking about it

. . . it can't be more than five minutes away! Come on, we can still get there in time, if I can work out the way!' She looked around, bewildered. It was nearly dark. 'Do you know how to get there?' she asked.

'I've been there already,' Edie said, exhausted.

'Brilliant! So you know the way!' Then, 'Hey!' she asked suddenly. 'Why did you leave?'

'Why did I leave?' Edie repeated slowly. 'I left, Janet, in order to find you. And now—' But something in Janet's expression quenched what remained of Edie's anger. *Do you want to be part of something larger than your stupid little world at Knight's Haddon?* She remembered her earlier resolution. 'I'll come with you,' she said, after a pause.

'Of course you will!' Janet said. 'Come on! I promised the others I'd help, but if you don't get a move on we'll be too late.'

'Promised you'd help?' Edie stopped and leant against a tree, looking at Janet with breathless incredulity. 'So much for your promises! I told them you were lost and none of them gave a monkey's! Why didn't any of them come with me to find you?'

But Janet did not share Edie's indignation. She behaved as if the whole incident by the river had been little more than a game of hide and seek.

'Edie, stop playing the blame game. I was the dolt, chaining myself up on the wrong side of the woods! I should have realized the camp had moved on. Anyway, what's it matter?' she reasoned cheerfully. 'I've got you. Now, which way?'

It was nearly dark when they arrived back at the clearing from which Edie had set off earlier. The camp looked empty, but the woods beyond were filled with flashing lights, and they could hear sirens shrieking.

'Come on!' Janet whispered, her face glowing – but as they were about to run across the camp two policewomen suddenly emerged from a tent.

'Hey, what are you doing here!' one of them shouted. 'You need to get back, there's a demonstration going on.'

'But we—' Edie began.

'Shut up!' Janet hissed, dragging her into the trees. They ran back on themselves, looping under cover around the clearing. Edie heard shouts, and fancied they were being followed – then she saw red lights burning through the woods ahead, as if a sunset had set everything ablaze. A little further on the trees thinned out, showing a barricade of bulldozers and trucks and two enormous cranes, and lights everywhere – torches, spotlights, flares – mocking the moonless sky.

In front of the vehicles was a chain of police officers, with crowds surging at them angrily from either side.

'Come on!' Janet urged, but the scene had a hideous, battle-like quality that rooted Edie to the spot.

Then from somewhere on the ground a spotlight started rotating, looping in huge, blinding circles, and as it swept over the vehicles Edie saw a line of men – six, seven or more – chained to the cranes, while police swarmed around them, holding what looked like toy rifles.

'Stop! What are they doing?' Edie shouted. 'They're

shooting them, they're—'

'They're Taser guns, stupid. Like stun guns. They give electric shocks,' Janet explained matter-of-factly. 'Come on, Wilson, don't be scared. They won't use them on us!'

Edie followed Janet across the field. But to her relief there was no chance of getting near to the vehicles – the police were keeping the crowds back.

Then, 'Hey, look over there!' Janet whispered, ducking her head.

Edie turned, and saw a sight even more astonishing than the guns: standing deep in the crowd just a few paces from them was Miss Fotheringay, addressing two policemen in her signature voice of steel:

'Unhand me! How dare you! I told you – there are children up there! Two of *my* girls! They are minors, and must be released at once. Halt the operation if you please. At once!'

Edie ducked too. Miss Fotheringay had not seen them. Her eyes were fixed on the officers, addressing them like fifth-formers caught smoking in the woods.

'Step back this instant and let me through!' she commanded, as she tried to elbow a path through the police line.

'Wow!' Janet whispered. 'She's pretty good. Come on, let's get away before she sees us!'

'Wait!' Edie said. 'What are they doing?'

The girls watched in astonishment as the officers seemed to move in and seize the headmistress by her coat. A torchlight glared on Miss Fotheringay's face, showing her startled expression as she flung out an arm;

~ 251 ~

then something flashed through the air – a stick, a truncheon, Edie could not see – and next thing there was a policeman on either side of her, dragging her away.

'She's been nicked!' Janet said, as Miss Fotheringay was bundled into the back of a van.

Edie watched stupidly as the doors were slammed shut. Miss Fotheringay had been arrested – because she had come looking for them!

'Stop!' she cried – as the van bumped out of the clearing, with its lights grinning.

'Cool or what!' Janet said. 'Did you see? She socked a policeman! Wow! Your darling Fothy's going to be in trouble now!'

What Happened Next

It was Sunday night, and it struck Edie that Miss Mannering's office was looking more than ever like a torture chamber, with its bleak metal shelves and harsh neon lights.

The door was closed, and blocked by the figure of Mr Robinson, standing with his arms crossed. And perched on the felt armchair by the unlit gas fire was Miss Pickering, her foot tapping nervously on the linoleum floor.

'So,' said Miss Mannering, her gaze fixed on Janet and Edie from behind her desk. 'You say that you saw Miss Fotheringay being escorted into a police van and driven away. What happened next?'

'No,' said Janet. 'That isn't what I said. She wasn't escorted into a police van – she was *dragged*. It was mental.'

Miss Mannering picked up a biro, and stabbed it impatiently into her notebook. 'I'll thank you to speak proper English, Janet Stone. And to answer my question, *what happened next?*'

Edie tried to throw Janet a warning look. An instinct told her that their story should be censored. But Janet seemed to have no such qualms:

'After Fothy—'

'Miss Fotheringay!' the Man interjected.

'Miss Fotheringay,' Janet conceded, grinning. 'Well once she'd been driven off, we wanted to carry on the fight—'

'*Carry on the fight?* You make it sound like a wrestling match!'

'It was!' Janet's eyes were shining. 'Oh, you should have seen Fothy – sorry, Miss Fotheringay – she was awesome! She wanted to get through to the cranes, that's where the people were being fired at by Taser guns, you see, and I suppose that's where she reckoned Edie and me would be—'

'Edie and I,' Miss Mannering corrected her, listening with a composed, yet somewhat baffled expression.

'Whatever,' said Janet 'but the police weren't letting her through, so then—' Janet stepped back from the desk, and swung out her arms with zeal. '*Unhand me! Let me through!*' she cried in a passable imitation of Fothy's low and carrying voice. '*My girls are part of that demonstration!* Oh, you should have seen her – she was the best!'

Edie winced. Could Janet not see that Miss Mannering was un-amused?

'I am not interested in Miss Fotheringay's conversation with members of the constabulary,' the deputy cut in sharply. 'Miss Fotheringay will be perfectly capable of relating that herself. I want to know *what happened next*.'

'Next thing we found Miss Pickering,' Edie said hastily, thinking it best not to report Janet's vain attempts to spin out the adventure by wriggling through the police lines. 'She found us just a few minutes after Miss Fotheringay had gone, and then—' Edie paused, her eye drawn to the curtainless window behind the desk and the black night beyond. They had been back at school for barely half an hour, but the day's adventures had already taken on the semblance of a dream. 'Then we got into her car, and we all came back to school,' she finished feebly.

'I see,' Miss Mannering said, folding away her spectacles. She sat silently a moment, staring at her desk. Then – 'Have either of you anything else to add?'

Edie looked furtive. They had not told Miss Mannering about their ordeal beside the river – and somehow Edie could not face having to relive it now. If the story was ever to be told, then she wanted Fothy to be the first to hear.

'What – what about Miss Fotheringay?' she asked quickly, fearing Janet might suddenly embark on the tale of the swollen river herself. 'Is she . . . all right?' She looked at Miss Mannering hesitantly – before turning in appeal to Mr Robinson, then Miss Pickering; but no one replied.

As her eyes roved the silent faces she was suddenly haunted by a memory of something Aunt Sophia had said one night over Christmas at Folly, when Edie had stalked out of the kitchen following a row with Lyle. 'Do what you like, I don't care – I'll be going back to school next week,' Edie had said.

'Well, make the most of it there, darling, I gather your darling Miss Fotheringay might not last long,' Aunt Sophia had replied. 'Poor old Fothy. I gather the governors aren't too pleased with her – Charles says they find her ways a bit autocratic.'

'Cousin Charles would say that!' Edie had said contemptuously, slamming the door.

She had given little thought to Aunt Sophia's snide, throwaway remarks. Her aunt was always sniping about Miss Fotheringay – and besides, Edie wasn't even sure what governors were. But she wondered about them now – and what they would say when they discovered that the headmistress of Knight's Haddon had been arrested.

'We – we haven't got her into trouble . . . have we?' she asked, looking at Miss Mannering plaintively.

'Miss Fotheringay telephoned me from the police station,' Miss Mannering said, looking at Edie with the ghost of a smile. 'She has been assisting the police in their enquiries, and should be allowed back to school shortly. She was relieved to hear that you were both safe.'

'Wow! Will she get a criminal record?' Janet asked eagerly – to which the Man gave her a scornful stare.

'A criminal record?' Edie asked in a frightened voice.

'I told you, Edith, there is nothing to be concerned about,' Miss Mannering said, looking in agitation at her phone.

But then the door suddenly swung open – straight into the back of Mr Robinson, who spun round sharply, but when he saw who it was he hurriedly stepped aside.

Miss Fotheringay swept into the room with an air of imperious dispatch, despite a rather crumpled appearance. She looked around, frowning, then her eyes fell on Edie – and softened.

'Caroline!' Miss Mannering began, visibly relieved.

Miss Fotheringay looked at her deputy and then at the clock above her head. 'Eight o'clock already!' she exclaimed. 'I'm so sorry, I had no idea. I got a bit tied up,' she added lightly, rubbing her wrists with her hands.

'Gracious, Caroline, are you hurt?' Miss Mannering asked.

'Just a handcuff bruise,' Miss Fotheringay said, lowering herself into the chair that Miss Pickering had vacated. 'They really shouldn't be allowed.'

Miss Mannering murmured sympathy – 'Beastly things' – while Miss Pickering, who was hovering skittishly by the window, gave an audible intake of breath.

The headmistress sat silently a moment, frowning as she appeared to take in the scene she had interrupted – the bleak, harshly-lit room, the watchful presence of Mr Robinson and Miss Pickering, and the two children ranged in front of Miss Mannering's desk.

'I've just come from one interrogation, and it looks like I've stumbled into another,' she said, in a voice that did not sound wholly approving.

Miss Mannering cleared her throat. 'Janet and Edith have now given me their version of events. I believe,' she said, looking at them inquisitively, 'that they have nothing more to add.'

Edie shook her head, longing for Miss Fotheringay's intervention – but not daring to meet her eye. It was thanks to her and Janet that the headmistress had got arrested. What choice would the school have now but to expel them both?

'Edith?' Miss Fotheringay asked slowly – and without looking up, Edie felt the scrutiny of her searchlight eyes.

'I . . . no—' she began, wretchedly, glancing at Janet for help. But there was a peculiar expression on Janet's face.

'We haven't told you everything,' said Newgirl at length, into the silence. 'At least, I haven't. I want to tell you the story *my* way, and I haven't begun . . .'

Fothy Comes Clean

'So you're quite decided then?'

Miss Fotheringay looked across the room at her deputy. 'I don't think I have a choice. The poor child has nowhere to go.'

'She's got a mother.'

'Hardly.'

'Has she been in touch?'

'Oh yes.' Miss Fotheringay paused, mimicking Eustacia Stone's rat-a-tat voice – '*If you expel my daughter you may as well know she's going straight into care. I cannot deal with her at this distance. As for her father—*'

Miss Mannering laughed and put her hands to her ears. 'All right, all right, I get the picture. He's gone, by the way.'

'Who?'

'The father. The man called Stonor.'

Miss Fotheringay frowned. 'I thought he'd gone hours ago.'

'He did, but he didn't get very far. Alethea Prentice found him asleep in a ditch halfway down the drive.'

'Oh, for heaven's sake!' Miss Fotheringay's eyes flashed fire.

'I know,' said the Man. 'But Miss Prentice was fine about it. In fact—'

'What?'

'I'm afraid she may be a little bit taken with the fellow.'

'With *Stonor*?'

Miss Mannering nodded, looking at the headmistress with raised eyebrows.

'Just what we need,' Miss Fotheringay said grimly.

'Well, it hasn't happened yet. We'll cross that bridge when it comes. In the meantime, I do see your case that Janet had better stay here.'

'I'm glad we're agreed on that at least,' Miss Fotheringay said, throwing her friend a grateful glance. 'Though, of course, I wish in a way we didn't have to. She's never going to be easy.'

'No,' said the Man slowly. 'But the way she told her story was quite remarkable. She resisted every temptation to glorify her own narrative, and seemed determined to paint Edie as the heroine. I felt my own role was slightly underplayed.'

'Your role, Diana?'

'Well, if I hadn't suspended Edith Wilson she

wouldn't have been liberated to save the day – again.'

Miss Fotheringay looked about to protest, then smiled. Diana was teasing her – again.

'You do know that the other girls call her "Edie the Liberator"?' said the Deputy. 'That there's been a whispering campaign against her all term.'

'Yes, of course I know that,' Miss Fotheringay murmured. 'Poor child.'

'Do you accept, Caroline, that you are partly responsible for the difficult time she's been having?'

But Miss Fotheringay's thoughts appeared to be following a different turn. 'Edith Wilson can look after herself. Janet Stone, on the other hand—'

'Was bent on trouble,' said Miss Mannering firmly. 'You can hardly blame yourself for that.'

'I did wrong,' said Miss Fotheringay, 'in mocking her.'

Miss Mannering said nothing. Her friend's remorse was a rare event.

'My worry now,' the headmistress went on, 'is whether Edith, Anastasia and Janet will get on together. Two's company but three's a crowd.'

Miss Mannering looked thoughtful. 'Janet Stone is unusually grown-up, as well as foolish. And she is good at her books, as well as stupid at life. I wonder if you shouldn't move her up a year – she's got an October birthday, so she wouldn't be so much younger than the other girls in the Third.'

Miss Fotheringay looked at her with esteem. 'Genius!' she murmured, with a quiet exhalation of breath.

*

News of Edie's daredevil rescue by the river, and of Janet Stone's subsequent elevation to the third year, rushed through the school – and inspired plenty of wry comments.

'What do you have to do to get moved up a year at Knight's Haddon?' Phoebe asked Belinda on the way into lunch.

'Run away and chain yourself to a tree trunk,' Belinda spluttered gleefully.

But there were no jealous feelings among the second years. Janet was popular enough with them, but she was peculiar. There was a general feeling that she had never belonged.

Of much more interest was the news of the tower. 'The developers have withdrawn their application, and I am pleased to inform you that Knight's Haddon has been offered a five-year lease on the building,' Fothy announced at Assembly on Monday morning. She did not offer a reason as to why the building project had been abandoned – but the girls spoke of little else.

'It's obviously because of the protesters,' said Rose, holding forth on the second years' table during an unusually noisy lunch. 'And two Knight's Haddon girls helped save the day, or rather the tower! Of course Fothy couldn't admit it though, because of all those horrid things she said about activists being pointless and potty.'

'Oh, come on, Fothy must have changed her tune,' Sally said excitedly. 'You heard what Janet said, about her standing up to the police – it sounds amazing.

Apparently she punched one of them, and knocked him flat!'

'I thought Janet said the police knocked *her* flat—'

'Yes, but that was only after she'd thumped one of *them*! That's what Janet said!'

But Janet was sitting at the third year table now, so it was left to Edie to set the record straight.

'She was brilliant – she just . . . just went potty,' Edie said, happy to let the rumours fly on.

'Oh, I wish I'd been with you in the woods, Edie,' said Belinda in a wistful voice.

'I don't,' Rose shuddered. 'I wouldn't have been brave enough.'

'But I wasn't brave,' Edie protested. 'I didn't have a choice.'

'Yes you did!' Anastasia said loyally. 'You hitched a lift to the action. We all know your story now, Edie! You can't hide.'

Edie shook her head. 'Janet was the brave one,' she said. As she spoke she looked at Anastasia warily.

'Edie the Brave, and Janet the Mad,' Anastasia replied – but her smile told Edie that Janet had been forgiven. Anastasia had at last accepted that her ferrets would be at home in the wild – it was where they belonged.

Also, although Anastasia was often unreasonable, she understood Janet's feelings of abandonment by her parents. As for Edie, in the woods she had seen a side of Janet that she would never forget – a courage that made Edie proud to be her friend.

But she knew Anastasia was relieved that Janet had

been moved up a year – and, secretly, Edie was relieved too. She wouldn't have been completely confident of their chances as a threesome.

'Whatever you say, Edie, I'd always have been frightened that she'd try and steal you from me again,' Anastasia said, as they were leaving the dining room.

'I don't think that was ever her plan,' Edie replied reasonably.

'The trouble with you, Edie is that you're too kind. You want to think well of everyone. Anyway,' Anastasia went on, before Edie could argue with this analysis of her character, 'it so happens I think well of Janet too, for the way she supported the protest. The way you both did.'

'And Fothy too,' Edie said loyally. 'Oh, Anastasia, isn't it brilliant that your father's backed down?'

But here a shadow crossed Anastasia's face.

'What is it?' Edie said. Anastasia had been dreading her mother moving into the tower – but now she looked uncertain.

'Of course I'm pleased,' said Anastasia slowly. 'But – Edie, you won't ever tell people, will you?'

'Tell them what?' asked Edie in mock innocence.

'Don't tease me! This is too important. I couldn't bear anyone to know that Papa was the one who bought it. Can you imagine, Edie, how they'd all start talking about "Anastasia's Tower", and I'd feel even more— Oh, God!' she said passionately. 'I'd just hate it!'

'Why? We used to call it "Helen's Tower".'

'That was different,' said Anastasia. 'Helen fitted in.

~ 264 ~

She wasn't an outsider, like me. Edie, please. Will you promise not to tell?'

'It's our secret,' Edie smiled. Then, 'By the way,' she said, 'it's all very well your father giving the school a five-year lease on the tower, but what's he going to do after the five years are up?' She calculated. 'We'll still be here you know – in the Upper Sixth!'

Anastasia looked at her slyly. 'You know Papa, Edie – by then he'll probably have bought the whole school, and tried to make Mummy our matron!'

Edie wished she could forget what Cousin Charles had told her about the prince paying her school fees. She loved Prince Stolonov, but some part of her resented his ability to arrange the world to his convenience. She felt mean-spirited to mind so much, and she still hesitated to mention the issue of her fees to Anastasia.

Miss Fotheringay, however, was more observant.

'What is it, Edith?' she asked, two weekends later when she and Edie were driving to Sunday lunch with Miss Fotheringay's father. 'I hope you're not sorry that I've moved Janet up a year. I hoped it would be easier for you and Anastasia to settle down again without her shadowing you.'

'Was that why you did it?' Edie asked. 'Do the Stolonovs have to be placated at every turn?'

'Whatever do you mean?' Miss Fotheringay asked, clearly startled. When Edie said nothing, Miss Fotheringay pulled in beside the road, and turned off the engine. 'Tell me what's bothering you, Edith. I can't help, if you won't tell.'

Her words struck a weary chord. Telling and not telling, sometimes telling or never telling. Edie was sick of the whole subject. Why not tell? Who would she be betraying?

'There's something I need to know,' she demanded, finally. 'Does Anastasia's father pay my school fees?'

Miss Fotheringay responded to this query with a look of such affectionate pity that Edie forgot her reserve.

'That's what Cousin Charles told me,' she blurted, 'when he picked me up after I'd been suspended. He said I should remember it, like . . . like I was still Anastasia's servant – and that I should know my place!'

'You poor child,' said Miss Fotheringay. 'It doesn't work like that. The prince has simply donated money to fund a bursary. He wanted it to be earmarked for you, but naturally I told him that would be quite improper. I couldn't have him in charge of your destiny.'

'So who is in charge?' Edie asked. 'I mean, who decides that I stay here – on this . . . this bursary?'

'I do, Edith,' Miss Fotheringay said. 'And I'm never going to let you go.'